NUR

Nurse Kate Trelawney is enjoying her private nursing assignment at a villa on the beautiful Greek
island of Corfu, until the presence of the supercilious
French doctor Laurent de Kerouac threatens to cast
a cloud over her Mediterranean idyll . . .

*Books you will enjoy
in our Doctor–Nurse series*

NURSE OVERBOARD

BY
MEG WISGATE

MILLS & BOON LIMITED
London · Sydney · Toronto

First published in Great Britain 1983
by Mills & Boon Limited, 15–16 Brook's Mews,
London W1A 1DR

ISBN 0 263 74378 0

Set in 11 on 11½ pt Linotron Times
03/0883

Photoset by Rowland Phototypesetting Ltd
Bury St Edmunds, Suffolk
Made and printed in Great Britain by
Richard Clay (The Chaucer Press) Ltd
Bungay, Suffolk

CHAPTER ONE

KATE Trelawney made her way through the jostling throng until she stood before the Trinidad steel band. The music was infectious and people in the crowd were moving their bodies in time to the irresistible rhythms, smiling at each other with faraway expressions on their faces. The atmosphere created by the simple calypso harmonies was one of azure seas, waving palms and warming sunshine—a marked contrast to the winter weather attire of the onlookers. She found herself caught up in the mood and willingly accepted the glossy holiday brochure held out to her by an eager girl.

'Holiday of a lifetime, you know,' said the girl. It was a well worn phrase, but obviously a valid description in this case, thought Kate wistfully as she gazed down at the idyllic tropical scene pictured on the cover. A Caribbean holiday would be really lovely to look forward to, especially in view of the chill January weather which awaited her outside.

She had decided to visit the London Boat Show on an impulse, for the Earls Court Exhibition Hall was just a step from where she lived. Her two flatmates had both gone home for the weekend to visit their parents and she had found herself with an empty Sunday. It was the last day of the Show and although the atmosphere was artificial, it certainly provided a foretaste of warmer days to come, with its colourful display of yachts, wind surfers and summer clothes.

Kate had been brought up in Devon, in the beautiful town of Salcombe, where water and boats had provided a constant backdrop to her childhood. She and her elder brother had spent many happy hours sailing the family's Salcombe Yawl, exploring the unspoilt Devon creeks and inlets. Their father was a retired Naval man with a deep-rooted love of the sea. In fact, it was almost certainly his influence which was responsible for the wanderlust she often felt. As a little girl she was always poring over the family atlas, seeking the faraway places from whence came the constant stream of letters and postcards generated by his career.

Thereafter had come the school trips and eventually the excitement of holidays abroad on her own and with girl friends. She was really quite well-travelled for someone in her mid-twenties, she reflected, feeling the old familiar restlessness stir within her.

The group of young people running the Caribbean Holidays stand were now showing every sign of turning the last hours of the Show into a party. The steel band was in full swing, several of the girls were dancing and Kate caught a glimpse of some wine being poured. She felt a slight pang of envy at their high spirits, but they were obviously celebrating the end of a job well done. It would be hard work, staffing an exhibition stand—on one's feet for hours at a stretch. Not unlike nursing in that respect, she mused, making her way through the assortment of gleaming hulls, crisp white sails and varnished timbers.

Turning a corner between the exhibits, she came upon a yacht of quite outstanding grace and beauty. The classic lines of the hull rose above her, looking curiously out of place in the land-bound setting. She searched for details of its designer and builder.

Of course. A *Nautor Swan*. An ocean thoroughbred, from one of the best yards in the world. It was a design her father spoke of with great respect, but the limitations of a Navy pension, even that of a retired Commander, meant he would never own one. She noticed that the price was significantly missing from the yacht's displayed specification, and she felt drawn to examine the craftsmanship closely. She made her way up the specially constructed stairway to the cockpit. The yacht was less crowded with visitors than other exhibits—further evidence of its high price. However, there was no harm in looking, she thought, as she smilingly acknowledged the attendant's request to slip off her tan leather boots and leave them on the stairway before stepping carefully aboard.

The quality of the finish was an indication that no expense had been spared in fitting out. She surveyed the shiny fittings and the tall mast rising impressively from the roof of the forecabin. She admired the superb carpentry of the closely laid teak deck and imagined the slender bow cleaving through the blue waters of some distant ocean, the spray flying and dancing in a tropical sun.

On an impulse, she turned and, reversing herself, placed a backward-stepping foot on the companionway steps down into the cabin, preparatory to investigating the interior.

'*Non! Prenez garde!* It's not fixed.' A shouted warning emanated from below and she realised too late that the step on which she had placed her stockinged foot was not in fact supporting her weight. The companionway ladder slipped from under her and she found herself suspended on the hand rails, her right foot twisting painfully. She cried out and hung there, humiliated and helpless.

A pair of strong arms gripped her beneath the shoulders. 'Let go and I will take your weight,' a voice said in her ear. 'Do it!' came the insistence as she hesitated. She was aware of the aroma of an expensive eau de toilette.

The pain in her ankle was intolerable and she had no alternative but to comply with the commands of her unseen rescuer. With an undignified scramble she found herself placed gently upright on her feet in the cabin. She turned to face the owner of the supporting arms.

A pair of piercing dark eyes inspected her from beneath sharply defined black eyebrows.

'An interesting method of entering a cabin.' The words were accompanied by a mocking gleam in the eyes. 'When moving around a boat, it is usually best to make sure equipment is secure before entrusting oneself to it.'

The implication that she was nothing more than a helpless female sightseer and the disturbing effect of his gaze stung her into an angry retort. 'The boats *I* am used to normally have such basic pieces of equipment as companionway steps properly secured in the first place,' she retorted, feeling her colour rising. Determined to exit from the situation with dignity, she wrenched her forearm from the firm grip which still supported her and turned to leave.

A sharp pain stabbed her right ankle and she winced, reaching out again for the handrails. 'I think I must have sprained my ankle,' she gasped.

'Here, sit down and let me look.' He was at her

side and she felt the muscles flexing in his arm as he helped her hobble across the cabin floor to a side berth.

'Can you manage, sir?' The cabin contained another, younger man, fresh faced and anxious.

'Yes, thank you. I am a doctor.' He eased her gently down on to the soft, luxuriously fitted upholstery. 'I think, mademoiselle, it would be better if you laid back while I examine your ankle. If we could just lift your legs up, so—' Before she could resist, he had raised her legs up on to the bunk.

'But I don't think that will be necessary and anyway I—'

Unheeding of this rather faint protest, he had cradled her foot in his hand and she was aware of gentle fingers probing her ankle. In the enclosed cabin, his examination seemed oddly unclinical— almost intimate. Feeling a need to dispel this ridiculous notion, she made to draw her foot away from his grasp, but he misunderstood the gesture.

'Painful, yes. I am sorry, I did not mean to hurt you. And beginning to swell already, you see. Can you bend your toes back towards you? Good. And press against my hand, so?' His brown eyes held hers for a moment and then returned to his examination, firm hands flexing the joint. She winced as he encouraged the furthest limits of its movement.

'Yes. I think we have a slight sprain here. No fracture. It would not have been possible to damage the ligaments badly with the mild twist you gave it.' He had taken the situation over entirely—a fact which she somehow resented.

'Yes,' she ventured. 'I agree. In fact, I'm a trained nur—'

Again he interrupted her. 'I am glad we agree.'
Amusement had returned to illumine the depths of
his brown eyes. She realised that, absurdly, she was
nodding. She straightened up, away from the back
rest of the bunk cushions, stung by his condescending tone.

'I have to get home,' she said. 'My boots, they're
outside on the—'

'Oh, but I think the swelling is too bad for you to
easily put your boots back on,' he announced. 'Of
course, we could try . . .' He paused.

'Oh no,' replied Kate hastily, her adamant re-
fusal springing more from the disturbing thought of
his gentle hands slipping her leg into the soft leather
of the boots than from an agreement with his
medical prognosis. It was all so embarrassing. He
was regarding her again and she had the distinct
impression he was reading her thoughts.

'I will lend you my support as far as the taxi rank,'
he announced magnanimously. 'It is not a great
distance to negotiate—even in your stockinged
feet.'

She glared at him helplessly but he seemed im-
pervious to her indignation. His eyes glanced over
her slender legs and she felt oddly vulnerable. Her
fingers found the hem of her skirt and tugged it
down to cover her knees.

'If you could wait a short while. I have some
business to complete with this gentleman,' he said.

The other occupant of the cabin was, she realised, probably deriving considerable amusement
from her discomfiture and the high-handed manner
in which she was being treated. He was obviously
some representative or other from the boat-
builders and was showing some deference to her

self-appointed deliverer. The latter had turned and was locking the companionway steps back into position.

'Yes, it was the engine specification I was concerned with. We were inspecting it just before our visitor so unexpectedly joined us.'

'Yes indeed,' she thought, 'inspecting the engine *and* failing to properly fit back the companionway steps afterwards.' Kate glared at the back of his head, but he was deeply immersed in talk about auxiliary diesels and horsepowers and similar incomprehensible jargon.

He spoke perfect English but there was a distinct overlay of an accent. French, she mused, and nodded to herself in confirmation as she remembered his shouted warning at the start of her mishap. She felt her cheeks growing hot again at the thought of her predicament.

What a ridiculous situation to have got into. She was confident about getting home once she was ensconced in a taxi. But it was making her way from the boat to the cab rank which concerned her—and the fact that she would need a helping hand from this rather overwhelming Frenchman in order to extricate herself from the cabin.

However, it seemed she had little choice. She resigned herself to her plight and leaned back, inspecting her surroundings. After all, a desire to investigate the interior of the *Swan* had been the cause of her downfall, literally, in the first place. From her vantage point on the side berth she could see the sleek lines of the teak woodwork running up to another cabin further forward—and aft to a neatly fitted galley, complete with cooking stove and storage lockers. Opposite her was a chart table

over which the two men were hunched, discussing
nautical matters and consulting lists.

He was tall, dressed in a Guernsey sweater in
dark French blue. A husky jacket was draped
across broad shoulders which supported a head of
dark crinkly hair. He was wearing cleanly tailored
slacks and a pair of stylish moccasins. He looked to
be in his mid-thirties, but had a youthful air about
him, which she had to admit blended rather attrac-
tively with his maturity.

'Well, that seems perfectly in order. You're sure
you can obtain the radio transmitter I have speci-
fied and can fit it here—so?' He pointed towards
some shelf space above the chart table.

'Yes, sir. Quite certain—and we'll have her road-
shipped out to Monte Carlo for you to collect at the
end of February.'

'Good. You have a note of my bankers, I believe.
The balance for completion will be through from
Paris in a day or so.'

'Thank you, Dr de Kerouac.' The young man
was gathering papers. They shook hands and he
turned to her again.

'Well, I suppose we must now attend to a safe
delivery of a different sort.' The mocking tone had
returned to his voice. Kate pressed her lips together
angrily and determinedly swung her legs off the
bunk. She rose to her feet, willing the pain in her
ankle not to disable her.

'I can manage,' she hissed through clenched
teeth and faltered towards the companionway.

'I do not think so,' he insisted and he was right,
for the steps were beyond her strength. A strong
arm encircled her waist.

'Now—a little hop and a jump and—*enfin!*'

Somewhat tousled and breathing rather more quickly than normal, she regained the cockpit. He stood at her side whilst she retrieved her boots and handbag held out by the attendant.

'Thank you. Now, I really can manage.'

'Again, I do not think so.' He was looking at her and she had the distinct impression he was enjoying her discomfiture. In her stockinged feet he seemed even taller.

He indicated the stairway leading from the cockpit down to the ground. 'In fact, a quick and simple solution is required.'

Before she could protest, he had again slipped an arm round her waist, stooped swiftly and, with the other arm under her legs, effortlessly lifted her off her feet. She groped hurriedly to press her flared grey skirt against the backs of her thighs, as, in one fluid movement, he stepped over the cockpit coaming and swiftly negotiated their way down the stairs. At the bottom, he stood, still holding her in his arms, his tanned face a mere foot from her own.

Colour suffused her cheeks as she registered the amused looks of several onlookers. A group of youths initiated a ripple of applause.

'Put me down,' she snapped, hot with embarrassment.

He gently did so and she stood, trying to regain her composure, but still obliged to favour one foot and retain the support of his arm.

'Come now. Can you manage to hobble a short distance? The cab rank is in that direction.' He nodded towards an exit, mercifully close.

'Yes, I think so,' she replied, thankful that at least they were now causing less interest amongst the passers-by. 'After all, I've only pulled the annular ligament. It's nothing really.'

'Ah, I see you have studied first aid.' He regarded her quizzically and she made to retort for the second time that she was in fact a fully qualified SRN. But his attention had shifted and the protest stilled in her throat.

As it turned out, the journey to the cab rank was quite easy. She was able to limp along, continuing to use his forearm for support. With his other arm he gently but firmly cleared a way through the crowd. 'Will you be able to manage at your destination?' he asked, leaning in through the cab door as she sank thankfully back in the seat. For a moment she thought she saw a flicker of concern in his deep-set eyes. It really made him quite attractive.

'Oh yes, thank you,' she replied. 'It's a ground floor flat—and there's a convenient railing.'

'I'll see the lady all right, guvnor,' interposed the cabbie, who had observed her plight.

'*Bon.*' He nodded and turned back to her. 'Now, you must rest the ankle for a day or two. And you will need a crepe bandage, which you should keep on for a time after you resume using the joint. You must bandage it so, for maximum support.' He had lightly grasped her ankle again and was making figure-of-eight gestures.

Again she resisted the impulse to inform him that she had dressed countless sprains, to say nothing of fractures, but it seemed hardly worth it. All she really wanted now was to escape from this ridiculous situation into the sanctuary of her flat. But there was still a parting shot to come. 'Well, *au revoir*,' he smiled and then said, patronisingly, 'and do not forget, if you are ever aboard a boat again, exercise much more caution.' He raised an arm in farewell and, apparently satisfied with this final pronouncement, slammed shut the door. The cabbie let in the clutch and they drew away into the gathering twilight of the January evening, leaving him standing on the kerb.

Later on, having successfully negotiated the entrance to her flat with the help of the driver, she sat on her bathroom stool, ruefully scrutinising the by now quite swollen joint.

'Enforced inactivity for you, my girl,' she murmured and applied her nimble fingers to winding on a supporting crepe bandage. She might have to be absent from the clinic for a day or two. It should not need to be longer, for it was only a mild strain and once the swelling had diminished, the joint would soon get back to normal. She was pretty fit, after all, and regularly played squash with her flatmate, Sue, at the South Kensington Squash Racquets Club to which they both belonged. In fact, it was at the club that she had first met Graham, with whom she seemed to be spending an increasing amount of time lately. She suddenly remembered that they had arranged to go out to a dinner party with one of his colleagues that evening. They usually went out together on a Sunday after he had been playing rugby in the afternoon. She had better call him.

She finished the bandaging and neatly pinned it. She could already feel the benefit of the support it provided. She gingerly rose to her feet, gripping the sides of the wash basin.

No, it was pretty painful. She would have to ring Sister to say she would not be in tomorrow. She was currently working at the Cavendish Square Clinic, in the Health Screening Department—a preven-

tive medicine section, concerned with monitoring
the health of busy executives and senior Govern-
ment and Foreign Embassy staff. It was not exces-
sively demanding work from a nursing point of
view—her chief responsibilities were the administering of visual field and hearing acuity tests,
together with mammography and thermography
for women.

In fact it was very light work and a far cry from
her previous post in the Intensive Care Unit of
South Devon General. She had undergone her
basic training with the South Western RHA at
Exeter, comfortably close to her childhood home,
and had gone on to the South Devon where she had
worked on several wards before applying for a
position in Intensive Care. She had found it re-
warding work, but the constant pressure and strain
had begun to take its toll and she had decided to
move to a less exacting post before her efficiency—
and therefore her patients—suffered. There was no
stigma attaching to such a decision, for turnover on
Intensive Care Units amongst nursing staff was
traditionally high and the stresses widely acknowledged.

After answering an advertisement in the *Nursing
Times* and a successful interview, she had found
herself in the busy capital city, adjusting to many
changes in her working and social life.

Yes, she had better make some telephone calls,
she mused, inspecting her reflection in the bathroom mirror. She was a pretty girl of medium build,
clear-skinned with naturally golden-blonde hair,
which she kept in a neat, shortish style to frame her
oval face. Two widely-spaced grey eyes stared
back at her from under quite remarkably long

lashes. A slightly retroussé nose surmounted a sensitively-shaped mouth.

'Another fine mess you've got yourself into,' she said aloud to her reflection. Although that was hardly fair, she recalled. She could hardly blame herself for unsafe steps, left loose and unattached by loose and apparently unattached Frenchmen. She frowned fiercely at herself and resolved to dismiss the whole Boat Show excursion from her mind. An enforced day or two off was not such an unwelcome prospect and they would have no serious problem covering her absence at the clinic. She negotiated her way from one piece of furniture to another, towards the telephone.

The clinic greeted her apologies with sympathy and instructions not to return to work until she was fully recovered. Graham was a different matter entirely. Apparently a member of the opposing team had applied a rather heavy rugby boot to his shin and he was complaining bitterly about the bruises.

'Well, looks like we're both in the wars, old thing. But at least I am still mobile. Sorry you can't make supper at Samantha's. The gang will miss you. So will I, of course. Want me to send round a take-away Chinese meal?'

'No thank you,' laughed Kate. 'There's plenty of food in the fridge. I shall be fine. Quite looking forward to an evening with my foot up.'

'Well, take care, Katie. I'll try to get round to visit you tomorrow, although we've got a big presentation meeting on for the new Chantelle perfume campaign. Might go on for a bit. See you.'

Kate replaced the receiver with a rueful smile. Graham was a young advertising executive, forever rushing off to meetings and talking about 'dead-lines' and 'panics', but he was very amusing—and good company. He had provided a welcome short cut for her into a London social life. She had half hoped that he would have foregone the supper party too and come round for a pleasant evening together, but that was a typical man for you.

She had never had a really serious relationship. She was fonder of Graham than most of the chaps who had filled odd moments of her life so far, but apart from a fairly intense and completely normal crush on a senior registrar when she had been in training, no man had ever totally captivated her. On occasion she regretted this, but she was an outgoing, social sort of girl and life rarely dragged. Not that she was free and easy with her affections, for she had been brought up to recognise tradition-al values.

Some time later, sitting in front of the gas fire watching television, she heard Sue's key in the front door and her face appeared round the living room door, cheeks flushed from the cold.

'Had a nice—?' She stopped, eyes widening at Kate's strapped-up limb, which was propped up on the end of the sofa.

'Kate Trelawney! What on earth have you done?'

Kate explained, giving in to the temptation to rail on about idiotic Frenchmen and their airs and graces.

'You mean he actually had the nerve to suggest you were a landlubber? Your brother should have been there—or better still your father. He'd have made him walk the plank!'

Kate laughed. 'Yes, you're quite right. Anyway,

it could have been worse. No real harm done.' She paused. 'Don't suppose you fancy putting the kettle on? All this hobbling around has worn me out.'

'Absolutely. Definitely. Cup of tea's just what's needed.' Sue disappeared in the direction of the kitchen, nodding seriously.

It was nice to have such a good flat-mate, mused Kate. She and Sue got on well together. They were opposites really, for Sue was far more introspective than Kate and held a responsible job as a secretary in a law practice at Lincoln's Inn.

The two girls spent a quiet evening, gossiping about Sue's visit home and idly watching television.

The swelling in her ankle had diminished substantially by the following day and she was gratified when Graham paid her a visit in the evening, glad to see him after being cooped up all day on her own.

'How's it going, then?' he enquired, surveying her ankle.

'Oh, it's fine, thank you, Graham. The swelling's well down now and it only twinges if I put my full weight on it. Aren't you going to take your coat off?'

'Well actually, Katie, I'm going to have to dash. All hell's broken loose at the office. My boss has gone and pranged his car. He's quite seriously hurt. They've taken him into St Vincent's. He's got a suspected fracture of the skull, broken ribs and leg. I think it's been touch and go. Anyway, I've had to handle things on my own all day and I've got to take Felicity English, the Chantelle perfume marketing manager, out to dinner tonight so that we can finalise the spring advertising. It's frightfully important.'

Kate suppressed her disappointment. 'I do hope

your boss is going to be all right. Didn't I meet him and his wife at your Company Christmas Party? We chatted to them quite a bit, I remember. He seemed such a nice man, really genuine—especially amongst all those odd characters you seem to find in advertising. His wife must be very upset.'

'Oh, I expect he'll come through it OK,' replied Graham, rather airily, Kate thought. 'It's a big chance for me, you know. If I can pull off this Chantelle perfume campaign it'll do me an awful lot of good.'

'Yes Graham, I suppose it will. Well, don't let me keep you.' Kate suddenly found his company rather jarring. She enjoyed his lively personality, but he really could be very superficial.

'Well, cheers old thing. Give me a kiss for luck, then.' He leaned down and she allowed his lips to brush hers. She did not return his kiss with any warmth but he did not seem to notice.

'I'll give you a ring sometime,' he promised and she heard the front door slam and the crackling exhaust of his MGB in the street outside.

It was an odd relationship, she mused. He was really quite generous and she enjoyed the socialising she experienced in his company. She had been excited to discover all the special places in London, the interesting restaurants of every conceivable variety, from Greek tavernas to French bistros, and Graham seemed to know them all. She had been introduced to a world of trendy young people, but had found that she was quite able to keep up with the pace at which they all seemed to live.

This particular evening, however, she felt quite bleak. It rather seemed that London only wanted your company if you were being bright, witty and interesting. And that was not how she felt at all. For a moment, she almost wished she was back at home, in the friendly, comfortable family house at Salcombe.

Never really being one to enjoy just her own company, she was pleased when Sue arrived home from work, followed shortly by Liz, their other flatmate, and her boyfriend. Their insistence that she repeat the story of her drama at the Boat Show removed the pall of gloom which had threatened to envelop her and the evening ended on a much higher note.

Several days later, she was back at the clinic, picking up the threads of her routine. The sprained annular had soon returned to normal and she was thankful that her swimming and squash had kept her so supple. Her duties in the Health Screening section had somehow become rather mundane and she asked for a transfer to some work with a higher basic nursing content.

The clinic was not organised into wards in the traditional manner—Surgical, Medical, Gynaecological and so forth—but rather into intensive, intermediate and minimal care sections. As a result of her transfer request, she found herself moved to the rehabilitation section of the clinic's intermediate care unit, nursing a variety of patients, all in various post-operative conditions. She enjoyed the work and the days sped by, interspersed by occasional evenings out with Graham. These seemed to become less frequent, for she was aware he was working very hard.

She was reminded of his work one day when she noticed the name Jollison on the admissions list.

Surely that was the name of Graham's boss?

'Is that Paul Jollison, of the McCain-Jollison advertising agency?' she enquired of Sister.

'Yes, that's right, Nurse Trelawney. Do you know him?'

'Yes, but only slightly. A friend of mine works in his agency.'

'Well, he's lucky to be alive after a really dreadful RTA. We're admitting him this afternoon from St Vincent's. He's still very poorly. We'll put him in Room 37—perhaps you'd take care of that.'

Kate reflected on how small a world it was as she prepared the bed in the comfortable, modern room. She clipped temperature, pulse and respiration blanks into the hanging chart holders and checked the lockers and wardrobe space. Details of diet would accompany the patient from St Vincent's. She scanned the admissions advice and noted the need for skeletal traction, right leg. Mr Jollison was still wearing spine to sternum strapping to knit his fractured ribs and her eyebrows lifted at the emergency surgery he had undergone. He had suffered haemothorax as a result of his chest injuries and had been on a Cape ventilator in intensive care. He had also been severely concussed and there was some suggestion of retrograde amnesia.

She reported the readiness of the room to Sister and together they checked through the case history.

'We'll have to keep an eye on his respiration, Nurse. Traction on his leg means immobility. It's not a good combination with chest injuries and respiratory complications. There's always a risk of pneumonia. How old is he?'

'Not old, actually. Fifty-two last October.' Kate's pretty face frowned as she consulted the records.

'That's just as well. Still, a careful watch on respiration—and we ought to have him semi-recumbent if Doctor's happy with his rib fracture progress. And physio for deep-breathing exercises.'

Kate made a point of being in Reception when the ambulance arrived with her new patient. She had an idea that Mrs Jollison might accompany her husband and thought some reassurance would be welcome.

In this she was correct, for Mrs Jollison did remember her, despite the briefness of their meeting at the McCain-Jollison Christmas party.

'Oh my dear, it's so nice to see a familiar face. It's been a dreadful few weeks. I thought I'd lost him, you know.'

Kate sensed tears very close to the surface in Mrs Jollison's eyes. 'Ah, I see you've brought a case with his things,' she hurriedly observed. 'Why don't you make yourself comfortable here for a moment. Sara will bring you a nice cup of tea.' She received a nod of affirmation from their beautiful Indian receptionist. 'And I'll just pop upstairs and make sure he's comfortably settled in. Then you can come up, make sure he's happy and well looked after and we can unpack his things together. Don't worry. We'll have him up and about again in no time.'

Mrs Jollison's eyes registered gratitude and, satisfied that she had provided the necessary reassurance, Kate sped upstairs to supervise her admission.

CHAPTER TWO

SHE caught up with the porters just as they were wheeling her patient into his room.

'Hello, Mr Jollison. I wonder if you recognise me in uniform.'

He looked up at her, uncertainty clouding his eyes.

'I'm Nurse Trelawney. I came to your Company's Christmas Party—with Graham Browne.'

'Ah yes,' he murmured vaguely. 'Young Graham. Must have a word with him about Chantelle Perfumes.'

'Plenty of time for that when you're feeling better,' she interjected. 'I'm here to look after you now and the first thing is to make you comfortable in your new bed.' She motioned to the porters to transfer him across to the bed and busied herself straightening the draw sheet and plumping the pillows. She was not over concerned at his vagueness, for he could well still be suffering from concussion and he was probably under mild sedation. She checked the St Vincent's record. Yes—five milligrams of Diazepam at midday.

'There's nothing to worry about at all,' she assured him, deftly tucking the sheets in. 'You've been very poorly and we're going to make you better.'

'It's Kate, isn't it?' He was now regarding her with clear intelligent eyes.

'That's right, Mr Jollison,' she replied, pleased at the clarity of his memory. 'It *was* a good party,' she added.

'Glad you enjoyed it, m'dear. Glad you enjoyed it. Is my wife still about?'

'She's down in Reception. In fact, I think she could come up and see for herself that you're being well looked after. I can help her unpack your case. George will fetch it, won't you George?' She nodded at one of the porters. 'And then, when that's done, we'll have Doctor take a look at you and see if we can't have you sitting up a little. But I'm still going to have to put your leg into traction for a week or so—'

'Not that ball and chain again,' he complained, but with a good-natured note in his voice. 'I thought I'd left that behind at St Vincent's.'

' 'Fraid not. I expect you've been told, it was a nasty fracture.'

'Didn't need to be told, Kate. I'm lucky to be alive. The other driver just pulled out in front of me. I didn't stand a chance. He'd been drinking they say—but he got away with just cuts and bruises.'

'It's often the case,' sighed Kate. 'Innocent parties in Road Traffic Accidents are frequently the more severely injured. It's never fair.'

Mrs Jollison left the clinic a different woman to the worried and preoccupied soul she had been when she arrived. 'I'm so glad it's you who's going to be nursing Paul, my dear. It makes such a difference, you know. When I'm at home, I won't worry so much, because I'll imagine you straightening up his bed and making sure he's eating properly. He's not the most independent of men—always has needed a lot of looking after, despite being such a successful businessman.'

'Those with the toughest exteriors often turn out to need the more care,' replied Kate.

'That's very true, dear. You've a wise head on those young shoulders of yours.' She was regarding Kate intently.

'Well anyway, you mustn't worry, Mrs Jollison,' went on Kate, slightly embarrassed. 'You can telephone at any time, visit whenever you like. Now, has Sara 'phoned for a taxi for you?'

Satisfied on this point, Kate withdrew, leaving a grateful Mrs Jollison quietly awaiting her transport.

The weeks passed and Kate was gratified to see her patient progressing well. It was obvious he was in some discomfort from his fractured ribs, but he was soon propped up in a semi-recumbent position and any problems with respiration were thankfully avoided. Breathing exercises had been immediately prescribed, supervised by the clinic's physiotherapist, and leg exercises, out of traction, soon followed. He still had occasional moments of blankness and often could remember nothing of the events leading up to the day of his accident. He also complained of bright lights flaring across his vision sometimes when his eyes were closed, but Sister assured Kate that all this was to be expected. In fact, everything was going well and he was soon enjoying quiet spells sitting in a chair next to his bed.

The pursed expression on Sister's face and the accompanying rather peremptory 'Come along to my office, would you, Nurse. I wish to discuss Mr

Jollison with you,' therefore came as something of a surprise to Kate one morning. She followed meekly behind and into Sister's office.

'Sit down, Trelawney. It seems as though you're to go travelling.' She paused. 'Do you have any important personal commitments over the next two or three months?'

Kate's grey eyes widened. 'Well I, er, no, that is . . .' She trailed off, nonplussed by Sister's somewhat lofty tone and the nature of her question.

'As you know, Mr Jollison is a very successful man in his particular line of business and will be able to enjoy the benefits of an excellent convalescence. He and his partner have recently purchased a Company villa down on the Mediterranean and he is to go there to recuperate.'

'Well, I'm sure that will be very beneficial for him. But how does it involve me?' Outwardly calm, she could feel a quickening of her pulse, for despite Sister's rather frosty tone, or rather because of it, she had a flash of foresight as to her answer.

'You are to accompany him, Trelawney. Mrs Jollison has practically insisted. Made quite a nuisance of herself. You should expect to leave in a fortnight, as soon as we're ready to discharge him.'

Several overlapping emotions coursed through Kate's mind. The thrill of anticipation—for she loved travelling—was soon eclipsed by misgivings about the nature of her responsibilities. 'But he's nowhere near ready to be completely separated from medical back-up.'

'Precisely. That is the principal reason for my agreeing to the request. Your role will be to provide a link between the patient and a local physician. In addition, I understand there is a very good local hospital in Corfu town which you can fall back on in any emergency. Your chief role will be to supervise his ambulatory and respiratory exercises and ensure he achieves a controlled and progressive return to active life. The accommodation is already amply staffed for domestic requirements and transportation is available I believe.'

'But Corfu,' said Kate agitatedly. 'I've travelled quite a lot but I'm afraid I can't speak a word of Greek—'

'That apparently will not be a problem.'

'—and what about pharmacy requirements?'

'You will have access to that via the local physician's dispensary.'

'I see.' Kate leaned back in her chair, thoroughly dazed.

'Something of a surprise for you, Nurse.' Kate realised that this trite observation signified a slight softening of Sister's earlier disapproval. 'But I'm sure you can take the responsibility adequately and will do an excellent job. The fact that your first reaction was concern for your patient is commendable. It rather supports my judgment that you were a good choice for the role.'

Still stunned, Kate could only acknowledge this with a faint murmur of thanks.

'I think you should give yourself a fortnight to prepare, providing Mr Jollison keeps up his current rate of progress.' Sister paused. 'I take it you are in a position to accept the assignment?'

'Oh, of course,' stammered Kate. 'Er yes, thank you.'

'Good. McCain-Jollison are making all the travel arrangements. They will be in contact with you direct as soon as we give them a discharge date for

the patient. Mrs Jollison will be accompanying you
for the convalescence. I imagine you will also be
called upon to provide a little moral support for
her. She is a rather diffident woman, I have
observed. Not like her husband at all.'

After satisfying herself about a few further practical points, Kate withdrew from Sister's domain to
the relative sanctuary of the linen room, where she
tried to assimilate the enormity of the news.

She was confident she could handle the professional side of things, once she had satisfied herself
about local arrangements. This did cause her some
misgivings, since she had once been in Ibiza during
a rather unpleasant outbreak of food poisoning at a
nearby hotel and she had not been at all impressed
by the response of the local authorities. However,
that was Spain. With luck, Greek facilities would
be better. Assessing this would have to be her first
objective on arrival.

An image of stepping off the plane assailed her.
It was one of her favourite moments when visiting
foreign countries as you emerged from the air-
conditioned cabin to be engulfed in a blanket of
warmth. She sighed, imagining the contrast between the dank, chilly English February and the
kindly Greek spring. Two or three months! Safe in
the privacy of the linen room, she indulged herself
in a little dance of delight. She was bursting to tell
somebody her good news. Her flatmates would be
green with envy. And there was Graham. How
would he take it? Eventually, she gained control of
her bubbling exuberance and contained herself
sufficiently to get on with the rest of her day's
duties.

As it happened, she was able to learn how Graham would take it that very evening, for she was to accompany him to a musical show with his new Chantelle clients. She dressed with care, wishing to do justice to an occasion which he obviously saw as important. She had resolved to keep things to herself, so as to allow him to entertain his guests undistracted, but her excitement gained the upper hand almost as soon as she saw him standing in the theatre foyer, anxiously awaiting his party.

'Graham, guess what?' she burst out within minutes of checking her coat into the cloakroom.

His eyes ceased their constant surveillance of the crowd and met hers. 'What's all the excitement then?'

'I've been asked to take your boss out to the Company villa in Corfu to convalesce. Isn't it fabulous? You don't mind, do you? It's only for a month or two,' she went on excitedly.

'Mind? Why should I mind? If Jollison believes it'll help him get better, having a pretty young female around while he relaxes in the sun at the Company's expense, that's his right. He is the Managing Director, after all.'

'Graham!' The shock in Kate's voice caused several nearby heads to turn. 'What on earth do you mean?'

'Not now, Kate, there's a good girl. Here comes Felicity and her boss. This is a very important evening for me.'

Before she could say a word further, he was waving exaggeratedly to their guests, ushering them through to a box, where he had arranged for several bottles of sparkling white wine to be served.

From that moment on, the whole evening rapidly

deteriorated, as far as Kate was concerned. It seemed to her that rather an excess of wine had been provided and, although she sipped only one glass, preferring the stimulation and enjoyment provided by the show, this in no way deterred the others. The Marketing Director of Chantelle, she soon discovered, possessed a rather penetrating laugh, which she found increasingly embarrassing as the levels in the wine bottles dropped. Graham appeared to be enjoying himself enormously and was dividing his attention between the show and his lady client, with a great deal of emphasis on the latter.

Kate found herself almost looking forward to the end of the performance, which was a pity, for the show, a lively jazz entertainment, had more than lived up to the rave reviews it had received. When Graham shouted over the final curtain applause that they were all 'going on somewhere', her heart sank. 'Are you sure, Graham?' she said. 'It's a working day tomorrow and your guests may be tired.'

'Nonsense,' drawled the Marketing Director thickly. 'Let's make a night of it!' His eyelid drooped in a lascivious wink and she realised in horror that he was squeezing her knee. 'I've heard that you nurses like to paint the town red.'

She stood up abruptly and hurried to collect her coat, seething with indignation. Standing outside on the pavement, she managed to draw Graham to one side. 'I don't mind helping you entertain your hideous friends,' she hissed, eyes flashing. 'But I am not going to be pawed by that—that ghastly person. Nor am I going to be late to bed tonight. The clinic's very busy at present.'

Graham was swaying slightly and he leaned towards her. She could smell the wine on his breath.

'If the clinic's that busy, old thing, I'm surprised that they can spare you for a three month paid holiday in Greece. Ah, there's a taxi.'

Kate's mouth gaped in astonishment. So affronted was she that she found herself bundled into the cab before she realised she should have left him standing, there and then, on the cold grey pavement. She huddled back in the corner, miserable and rejected.

She was beginning to see Graham very differently. She had known that he was ambitious, but she had not realised he was prepared to compromise himself so much to further his career. He really was enjoying the company of these dreadful people. She cast a sideways glance at the girl. She seemed a colourless sort, obviously flattered by Graham's attentions.

The crunch came half an hour later, when she was dragged by their male guest on to the dance floor of a night club. What music there was appeared to be intended merely as an excuse for vertical clinches by several barely moving couples, including Graham and the Felicity English girl. Kate wriggled free and, muttering some excuse or other, grabbed her handbag from their table and fled. Pressing a tip into the hand of a passing waiter, with a request that he tell Graham she felt unwell and had left, she rushed out into the clean, fresh night air, pausing only to collect her coat at the entrance.

Fortunately, a cab was at that moment disgorging another bunch of late nighters. She scrambled into it, breathing a sigh of relief as it rattled her off homewards. She had a growing conviction that it was very unlikely that she would ever see Graham again. To her faint surprise, this realisation seemed in no way tinged with regret.

She set aside the following weekend for a visit home to Salcombe. It would be the last opportunity to see her parents for quite some time and there was the practical matter of where to leave her Renault 5 whilst she was away. She did not like the idea of her little car—a twenty-first birthday present from her parents—sitting in the uncertain security of the street outside her flat for two or three months. It would be far safer in Salcombe.

The Friday evening traffic was heavy and it took an hour or so to negotiate the Cromwell Road and the elevated section of the M4. Once clear of the city, however, she made better progress and was turning into the driveway of her parents' house well before eleven o'clock.

The contrast between her family's reaction and Graham's, on hearing about her forthcoming trip, could not have been greater.

'How marvellous, Kate,' beamed her father. 'The Mediterranean, you lucky girl. Blue water and sparkling weather. I was stationed out in Gibraltar as a midshipman, soon after the war. Had the time of my life—fabulous place for sailing. And Corfu is beautiful—'

'It's not a holiday, Dad,' interrupted Kate firmly, clasping her hands round her bedtime mug of cocoa and leaning forward on the comfortable family settee. 'Mr Jollison's been badly injured and he'll be quite a responsibility. Heaven knows what the local medical facilities will be like. In fact, it's all rather daunting.' She broke off and stared into space.

'I'm perfectly sure you will cope admirably, dear,' reassured her mother. 'You've always had a cool head and I don't think your patient's Company would pack him off anywhere second-rate to convalesce.'

Her father was lighting his pipe. 'I suppose this means you won't be around at Easter to help me with fitting-out *Lady Spray*,' he observed dolefully.

'I'm afraid not, Dad,' she replied with genuine regret. Helping her father prepare his ketch for the coming season's sailing was a regular event in her year's diary and one which she enjoyed.

'I was going to take a trip out to the mooring tomorrow, just to check her over and do a couple of odd jobs, if you fancy a breath of Salcombe sea air?' he ventured, an eyebrow raised.

'I'd really like that,' she replied.

Her weekend passed all too quickly, for she found herself pleasurably immersed in chores aboard *Lady Spray* for most of Saturday. She enjoyed her father's company, sitting on a bunk in the cosy cabin, putting a few well-needed stitches in some sails and splicing eyes into various pieces of rope. There was something very absorbing about boats, she reflected, realising that she had not given a thought to Graham all morning.

Of course, she could not tackle all the tasks aboard the ketch, for there were some that simply required the superior strength of a man. Her father was perfectly happy to let her try her hand at almost anything, however, and smiled approvingly as she expertly steered the outboard motor dinghy in and out of the moored fishing vessels, setting the buoys bobbing and the seagulls flapping, as they made their way back across the harbour at lunchtime. She had always felt that his willingness to let her experiment, especially in the nautical activities which he understood so well, had given her far more self-confidence than most girls could develop. She smiled warmly at him as he perched up in the bow of the dinghy against the background of higgledy-piggledy white Devon houses dropping down to the greystone quay.

She devoted most of Sunday morning to reviewing the wardrobe she would need in Corfu. She consulted with her mother and together they determined that a mixture of warm and cool outfits would be needed, since she would be experiencing a wide range of temperatures from Spring to Summer. A selection of light cotton dresses, together with summer sandals, casual tops and skirts soon filled a small suitcase. She would add to these the jeans and warm jumpers she kept at the flat, together with essential items of uniform. Lastly, and with firmly restrained ideas as to whether she would have any opportunities to wear it, in went the sleek black bikini she had bought last summer for weekend sunbathing on her parent's garden patio.

Her father offered to drive her up to the mainline station at Exeter after Sunday lunch and she gratefully accepted.

'Goodbye, Kate,' he called, blowing her a kiss as the Inter City express began to move off. 'Take care of yourself—' She smiled acknowledgement. '—And no falling in love with any Greeks.' A cry of protest died in her throat as she recognised the mischievous twinkle in his eye.

'Spoilsport,' she replied and waved back until a bend in the track took him from her view.

*　　*　　*

Somehow the journey back to London became merged into the far longer journey she was soon to make. The McCain-Jollison advertising agency handled all the travel bookings with impeccable efficiency, even organising part of her following month's salary to be paid in travellers' cheques. She realised with delight that her outgoings would be minimal, with the catering and domestic facilities that apparently went with the villa. Keeping the rent up on her share of the flat whilst she was away was certainly not going to pose a problem. She might even be able to afford to bring back some presents. Might even be able to save a little . . .

Fancies like these, however, were soon submerged beneath the practicalities of preparing her patient—and indeed his wife—for the forthcoming journey.

Paul Jollison had continued to make excellent progress under the first class aftercare of the Cavendish. His leg fracture had mended well and a small operation the week before their departure had removed the paraphernalia of skeletal traction. With the aid of crutches, he was now making short excursions about the clinic, but was still a little limited in these by residual pain from his chest injuries. Physiotherapy would play a major part in his convalescence and whilst Kate would lack the sophisticated equipment provided at the Cavendish, she was confident she would be able to cope.

Despite her patient's having technically become an ambulatory case, it was decided that he would undertake most of the journey with the added security of a wheelchair. McCain-Jollison had advised her that all necessary facilities to handle this would be provided by the airline. So it was that Kate found herself, with her patient and his anxious wife, speeding towards Heathrow Airport in the efficient luxury of a TransMedic International Citroen ambulance, one bright, blustery morning in March.

Aboard the aircraft, she smiled across at Mrs Jollison's apprehensive face as she tucked a blanket round her husband's legs. 'There we are. So far so good. Sorry it's an aisle seat, Mr Jollison, but I think you'd find it difficult to negotiate yourself across to a window seat.'

'To tell you the truth, Kate, I'm a touch blasé about flying. I seem to have done an awful lot of it over the years on business trips. It's far better for Mary to have the window. She'll enjoy the view. I'm afraid I shall probably nod off.'

'And I'll be sitting across the aisle, right here,' went on Kate. 'After I've returned the wheelchair to the departure gate, that is.'

'But won't we need it when we—?' Mary Jollison was leaning anxiously forward again.

'We're to be met at Corfu airport by local transport and all the necessary equipment. Don't worry,' Kate reassured smoothly. 'Now I'll only be a minute or two.'

If things continued to go this smoothly, she told herself as she reversed the wheelchair down the gangway, it really was going to be an enjoyable experience. Just what she needed, in fact. An excellent opportunity to shake Graham completely out of her system—not that he had ever seriously entered it, she now realised—and she gave a delicious shrug of freedom. Freedom was how it was to be these next few months. She had her patient to look after, his wife to be reassured and, in between, life was to remain uncomplicated.

The flight passed quickly and very soon she felt a slight popping in her ears as the big jet passed over the South-East edge of Italy, banked and began its long descent to their destination. Soon she could see the hazy coastline of the island through a cabin window as they swung into their approach path. A half-remembered quotation jumped into her mind from some poet studied as a schoolgirl—'*Corfu, spread like a shield upon the dark blue sea.*'

She hurriedly dismissed any tendency to day-dream and looked across at her companions to see that they had complied with the 'fasten seat belts' sign, but the Greek stewardess was already check-ing. The girl seemed haughty and had not offered them any extra attention at all during the flight. Not that she needed any, but a clearly disabled passen-ger, accompanied by a uniformed nurse, might have merited a little extra service—or at least the offer of it. Perhaps her English was not up to a lengthy conversation, thought Kate charitably, although a suspicion lingered that the girl resented her in some way.

She saw that Mrs Jollison's knuckles were white with the intensity of her grip on the seat's armrests as they entered the stomach-swooping jolt of land-ing and deceleration. Heavens, it did look as though the patient's wife was going to need more nursing than the patient, Kate thought as she waited for the mêlée of disembarking passengers to subside.

She peered out of a window and realised with a start that Corfu airport did not of course boast the constant-level walkways of Heathrow. The passen-

gers were making their way down a set of steps and
walking across the tarmac to a bus. She had not
thought to check the disembarkation procedure for
a disabled passenger in detail, relying on the
arrangements which she had been assured McCain-
Jollison had made. She turned her head aside from
her companions to hide her dismay that the aircraft
was now empty apart from the cabin staff clustered
in the galley, ignoring them.

With studied casualness Kate rose to her feet and
approached one of the stewardesses.

'Excuse me, I believe special arrangements have
been made for my patient—a wheelchair and—?'

'Yes. All is arranged. Wait please.' The girl was
ticking off items on some sort of inventory and
barely raised her head.

'But there are only the steps and my patient
cannot possibly . . .'

The stewardess looked up. 'All is arranged.
Many times we fly disabled passengers.' She gave a
haughty wave in the direction of the exit door.

Not fully comprehending, Kate made her way
forward, pausing on her way to make reassuring
noises to the Jollisons. She reached the doorway
and looked out, concern furrowing her face.

All she could perceive were a pair of approaching
vehicles which she recognised as baggage transporters. With sudden realisation, she recalled that this
was how less well-equipped airports handled
wheelchair cases—by treating them as rather inconvenient items of air freight.

Sure enough, she could make out a wheelchair
strapped on to the flat loading platform of one of
the transporters. The vehicle drew up and two
porters unloaded the chair roughly and then started

up the steps towards her, leaving it behind on the ground. She returned to the Jollisons, summoning far more breezy confidence that she actually felt.

'It's going to be an unusual method of unloading you,' she smiled, unclipping her patient's seat belt. 'You're going to be carried down to ground level by the baggage staff. How about that?'

Paul Jollison laughed aloud and forestalled an inevitable cry of concern from his wife by patting her hand.

'Looks like you and I are going to experience some exciting methods of getting around, Nurse Trelawney,' he added as she reluctantly made way for the unsmiling baggage porters to help him from his seat.

'I expect the final stage of our journey will be by pack mule,' he called as the men grasped each other's wrists and he was chairlifted down the steps, waving royally to an imaginary audience.

'Heaven forbid,' murmured Kate to herself, eyes raised, and made her way back to collect Mary Jollison.

By the time the trio emerged into the arrivals hall in the main airport building, Kate was hot, harassed and exceedingly angry. The combination of officious customs men, an unnecessarily long haul across the tarmac, without the assistance of the porters to push the wheelchair—it was not a lightweight model and she was sure it ought to run more easily—and the interminable wait for their baggage were burdens for which she had not been prepared. Fortunately, the Jollisons had the good manners not to voice complaints at her and simply preserved a sympathetic silence as she negotiated the difficulties and delays.

As a result, she almost fell with relief upon the shoulder of the grinning, rotund little man who approached them, flourishing car keys aloft between finger and thumb.

'Jolsons?' he mispronounced grandly. 'Spiro.' He thumped his chest in self-introduction. 'I drive you villa. Also I drive you baggage. Yes?'

Before she could reply, he had commandeered a trolley for them and was leading the way out through the exit doors. With relief, Kate saw that they were being taken over to a very large Peugeot estate car with a front seat which was easily accessible to Paul Jollison and a capacious interior into which they all fitted, plus cases and wheelchair, in comparative comfort.

She sank back thankfully in her seat as their driver negotiated them through the colourful bustle of Corfu Town, hoping heartily that the worst part of their journey was over.

CHAPTER THREE

GRADUALLY, as the groups of peasant women, laden donkeys and press of traffic began to thin out, Spiro's exotic style of driving and enthusiastic honking of his horn moderated and Kate began to relax.

They had taken the winding coast road North, its surface covered with a fine white dust which their progress lifted into a billowing cloud behind. Ahead, however, the scenery was touched with crystal clarity, for the Mediterranean spring was upon the island. Everywhere was the flutter of new leaves. Amongst the silvery shimmer of the olive groves, she could see that the gnarled old trees were covered in a mantle of creamy flowers. Here and there, tall cypresses lifted up against the sky, embellished with a decoration of light green cones. Along the edge of the road, in amongst the trees, were tumbled clumps of spring flowers, anemones, crocuses and marigolds, clustered together in cascades of colour, whilst in the background, the rumpled brown coverlet of the mountains brooded silently in the afternoon warmth.

'You like, yes?' Spiro waved theatrically to the world at large and the Peugeot plunged to and fro across the road like an erratic gazelle.

'It's beautiful,' Kate answered hastily and, seeking a means of keeping his attention on the road, pointed ahead to where the coast swung eastwards. 'Is that where we're going?'

'Yes, we go,' answered Spiro enigmatically. 'Netriti, we go Netriti.'

'The villa's in Netriti,' explained Paul Jollison over his shoulder. 'I am told it's a very pleasant spot, although I've never seen it.'

'Paul's partner, Ed McCain, handled the purchase of the villa for the company, you see,' said his wife.

'And the local doctor, he is in Netriti, too?' enquired Kate.

'Yes, we go Netriti,' answered Spiro.

She subsided into a frustrated silence. The road had begun to climb now, winding in and out of ravines and hills. Here and there, they caught a glimpse of the sea, blue as sapphire, moving closer and closer to their route. A signpost came into view on their right and Kate realised she was reading the Greek alphabet letters for Netriti. Spiro turned off the main road onto an unmade track, whose rough furrows the Peugeot's suspension handled with ease, negotiated a steep incline and halted on a tight hairpin bend.

'Villa Netriti,' he announced dramatically.

They peered forward and delightedly made out a white-walled building nestling amongst the olive trees. It was built in the shape of a square, with three sides enclosing a gravelled quadrangle. The fourth side consisted of a high wall, into which two large wooden gates, now open, were let. A red Alfa-Romeo stood in the courtyard, gleaming in the sun. Along the seaward facing wall, Kate could make out a verandah, hung with a dense pelmet of grapevine. It gave on to a neatly terraced garden, which dropped in a series of levels, thick with hyacinths and asphodel, to a low, crumbling brick

wall, which sprouted with mosses and ferns. Beyond
the wall a grove of lemon trees fell away to the glittering sea. It was quite breathtakingly beautiful.

The slight bump, as Spiro re-engaged the gears,
disturbed her reverie and she firmly brought her
attention back to matters in hand. The first priority
was to get Mr Jollison comfortably settled. She
gestured to Spiro to help her with the wheelchair as
they drew up. No doubt her patient could have
resorted to his forearm crutches, but she noticed his
face was somewhat drawn. The long journey would
have tired him and the stupid delays at the airport
must have added to the strain. She compressed her
lips with annoyance at the incompetence of the
promised local arrangements.

Her annoyance turned to a rare flash of anger as
she realised the impossibility of pushing the
cumbersome wheelchair across the loose gravel of
the courtyard. 'Honestly,' she burst out, 'this sort
of equipment went out in the fifties. It weighs a ton
and the wheels are too small. Can't we get hold of a
modern, lightweight one.' She glared at the unfor-
tunate Spiro.

'The doctor, he come,' he said hopefully.

'Ah yes, the doctor,' she said icily. 'I don't expect
he speaks English either. I certainly hope he at least
has some decent medical qualifications. The facilities provided so far suggest he has the professional
competence of a package tour operator.' She
paused as she realised that her three companions
were looking at her with peculiar expressions on
their faces. In fact, they appeared to be looking
past her and she turned to find the object of their
attention. A voice, speaking in English but with an
oddly familiar French accent, assailed her ears.

'Would seven years at University College Hospital, followed by postgraduate research at a Paris medical school, provide sufficient qualifications for you?'

He was framed in one of the windows opening onto the courtyard, leaning nonchalantly on the sill, wearing the same expression of faintly amused interest she had first observed on that well-remembered day in January. She gaped like a vacant teenager, totally lost for words. She could not even be sure he had recognised her in her uniform. The silence seemed interminable.

'*Alors*. I will join you.' He disappeared from view and emerged from an adjoining doorway.

'Mr Jollison I presume—and Mrs Jollison.' He was shaking hands. 'I am Dr Laurent de Kerouac. I have the welcome responsibility of ensuring that your convalescence here in Corfu is a successful one.' He turned to Kate. 'With the help of your delightful nurse companion, of course. Miss—?'

'Trelawney, sir,' she stammered. 'Katherine Trelawney.'

He had grasped her hand in a cool, firm grip. The intentness of his gaze caused her that strange sense of discomfort again, which turned to a feeling of resentment as his eyes swept down her trim figure and neat uniform. He had held her hand unnecessarily long and she snatched it away, acutely aware that she must look hot, flustered and travel weary.

A smile touched the corners of his mouth and danced briefly in the depths of his incredibly deep brown eyes.

'I have the impression we may have met before,' he said. 'Professionally of course. A collaboration over an ankle injury, I seem to recall.'

Mrs Jollison was about to break in on this almost intimate exchange when he turned and issued a stream of commands in fluent Greek. Spiro and he each took one side of the wheelchair and, in a moment, had successfully negotiated the gravel and were wheeling it over the paving of the quadrangle.

'You are quite right, Nurse Trelawney,' he called over his shoulder. 'This wheelchair is *une voiture formidable* . . . I will have a 1983 model sent out from my clinic in Corfu town.' He had stopped and was regarding her quizzically, for she still remained by the Peugeot, as though rooted to the spot. 'Do you not wish to inspect your patient's quarters?'

'Oh yes, of course,' she blurted and, recovering some measure of composure, grasped Mrs Jollison's arm and followed.

The doctor was leading the way along one side of the square building towards a doorway. She fell in behind with Mrs Jollison, her mind in a turmoil. Of all things to happen, to find herself having to work with a doctor to whom her very first introduction had been something she would rather forget—and with the circumstances of their second meeting also leaving much to be desired. Goodness knows what he must think of her. On the other hand, it had not been an easy arrival and she had been justified in complaining. He had even agreed with her about the inadequacy of the wheelchair. Still, it would be as well to try and make amends.

He had opened the door with a flourish. *'Voila! La chambre Jollison!'* He stood aside to let Mrs Jollison enter, followed by her husband being pushed by Spiro.

'Oh Paul, it's lovely,' Mrs Jollison exclaimed.

Kate followed on into the room, past the doctor's bow and extended hand of invitation. The room was large and cool, sparsely but tastefully furnished with two divan beds, wardrobes and cabinets. The floor was mosaic tiled with a large and beautiful rug, round which a comfortable suite of settee and easy chairs was grouped. An en suite bathroom was visible through another door. The room occupied a corner of the building with windows along two walls, through which the late afternoon sun was streaming. One set were of the floor to ceiling type and stood open, looking out on to the verandah she had observed from the road.

Mrs Jollison was opening and shutting cupboard doors and drawers like an excited schoolgirl, watched with an indulgent smile by her husband. 'It's just what you need, Paul,' she exclaimed. 'Lots of rest and relaxation in lovely surroundings. He'll soon be back on his feet, won't he, Kate?' She paused. 'But where is your room, dear?'

'Nurse Trelawney will be sleeping in the next room along the terrace, within easy call,' answered the doctor. He turned to her. 'Why don't you take a look while Spiro unloads your baggage?' He reverted with startling rapidity into further torrents of Greek and she followed the two men out of the room. Without a break in his conversation with Spiro, he raised an eyebrow at her over his shoulder and nodded firmly at another door. She lifted the latch and peered in. The room was smaller, but the same delightful qualities of light and space prevailed. Her eyes fastened on a raised platform at one end of the room. Two small steps rose to it and a low balustrade ran along its edge. A large flat mattress, made up with sheets, blankets and a pillow, occupied the surface of the platform. It could only be a bed, she realised, but one of the strangest she had ever seen.

She turned to the French windows and, opening them, stood looking out over the garden. The perfume of spring flowers and the frantic, ringing chorus of cicadas filled the air. She raised her eyes to the sea beyond the terraced garden. It seemed to be a channel of some sort, for she could see some dark, ancient looking mountains away across the shimmering water to the North-East. She shaded her eyes with her hand, looking into the distance.

'Albania,' said a voice close to her ear, startling her, for she had not heard him come in. She turned. 'Not a country renowned for its hospitality.'

'No, I've heard not,' she said. There was an awkward silence.

'And your room. You will be comfortable?'

'Yes, thank you. It will be reassuring for Mrs Jollison to know I am nearby.'

'I agree. She is an anxious lady. I have met her type many times.' They exchanged a look which she felt bordered almost on professional rapport.

Encouraged, she plunged on. 'I must apologise for the rather unnecessary remarks I was making out there when we first arrived . . . It had been rather a tiresome journey and—'

'Ça ne fait rien. I am not unaccustomed to young nurses occasionally becoming a little emotional. You will learn to control it.' He regarded her in a self-satisfied manner, looking for some reaction of gratitude for his forbearance.

Kate, however, only felt as if she were being patronised and continued with what she had been saying, but in a very different tone. '—in fact, a *very* tiresome journey, not helped at all by officious Greek immigration staff, hot and dusty delays and a driver who speaks as much English as I speak Greek.' She stopped, aware of twin spots of colour burning in her cheeks.

'As I said, a little emotional . . .' She had the feeling he was laughing at her again and struggled to regain her composure. '*Enfin.* I wish to examine the patient. You will accompany me please.' He moved towards the door but hesitated and turned to her again. 'But your room. You are happy with it, yes? You should be comfortable I think. The sleeping quarters are unusual, are they not? It is a traditional Greek bed. It is the only room in the villa which still retains one. You will sleep well on it, I assure you. I use one myself.'

She nodded, glad of the change of subject and walked over to it, placing a foot on the lower step and touching the carved wood of the balustrade. 'The villa is old, then?'

'Oh yes . . . and many generations of its inhabitants have been sired on that very bed.' He was looking at her with that penetrating gaze of his and she felt the colour rising in her cheeks again. 'However,' he added archly, 'it is most important to descend the steps carefully when rising. Backwards is best—not unlike descending into a yacht's cabin.' He disappeared behind the door, leaving her standing there, agape at his impudence.

His head reappeared round the door, startling her. 'I am glad to see your ankle is fully recovered, by the way.'

It was probably only the professional requirement of assisting him with his examination of Mr

Jollison that enabled her to conceal her feelings of confusion and she concentrated on clarifying certain aspects of her nursing assignment with him. Much to her relief, he had brought a comprehensive box of pharmacy supplies in the boot of his car and they checked them through together in her room. She had selected a wall cupboard for them and was pleased to see that he had catered for most eventualities.

'I will leave the administering of sedatives to your judgment, Nurse. Temazepam might be beneficial tonight, to help him get off to sleep in strange surroundings. There are some five-milligram Valiums also. Do you have any questions?'

'Yes,' she answered. 'I'm a little concerned about any emergencies. You say you are based in Corfu town. It seems a long way and we are rather isolated. I'm not certain how I . . .'

'Ah, but there is a telephone. Spiro will make any calls for you. And I can be here in an hour.'

'But as I said earlier, Spiro speaks hardly any English. And I'd like to know about domestic arrangements. Is his wife more fluent?'

'No, I'm afraid not. You will meet her when she serves dinner. Her name is Elena. It is a problem, I can see.'

'Well yes, I think it is. They said in London that there would not be any language difficulties.'

He had folded an arm across his chest. 'There is someone I know who passes here almost every morning, who could act as an interpreter for you, if you could save up your routine requirements from Spiro and Elena for one session every day or so. Would that be a help?'

'I'm sure it would—at least, until I get myself

properly organised and can find my own way
around. Thank you.'

'OK. I will arrange it for tomorrow morning. It
will be early of course, people have work to go to.'

'I'm an early riser myself,' said Kate firmly.

'*Bon.*' She thought she saw a gleam of approval
in his eyes. 'And now I must leave. I have an
evening surgery. I have asked Elena to serve supper for you all in the Jollisons' room. That way, our
patient can have his in bed, with your supervision—
and you and Mrs Jollison can relax and eat yours on
the verandah. That would be enjoyable, yes?'

Surprised at his thoughtfulness and the sudden
warmth in his voice, she smiled and nodded.

He turned and left her. She heard him knock on
the adjoining door and call to the Jollisons that he
would pay a visit at about the same time the next
day and, soon after, the fiery crackle of the Alfa-
Romeo's engine signalled his departure up the
winding track to the main road.

After the rigours of their journey, the evening
passed pleasantly and they were all able to relax
and enjoy the light supper which Elena and Spiro
served. Elena was a cheerful soul, like her husband, with a bustling air of efficiency. Kate took to
her immediately.

By the time they had eaten, the surprisingly short
Corfu twilight had passed and night had fallen.
With it came several barely stifled yawns from all
three of them and an early night was soon decided
upon. Making sure that her patient was comfortable, Kate noted his drooping eyelids and decided
against administering the sedative which Dr
Kerouac had suggested. It looked as though natural
tiredness would have its own effect. She extracted a

promise from Mary Jollison that she would be called for any reason whatsoever.

'Even if it's simply that he can't sleep,' she murmured. 'I'm just next door. Judging by the yawns, though, I think we're all going to have a good night's rest.'

With some relief, she went next door to her own room and gratefully changed out of her uniform. Slipping into her cool cotton nightie, she negotiated the steps up to her sleeping platform and slid down between the crisply laundered sheets. She stuck an experimental hip and elbow into the mattress. It was firm, to say the least, but not uncomfortable.

Her mind turned over the day's events and, despite herself, she again felt a prickle of embarrassment at being so inconveniently overheard on their arrival. The ubiquitous Dr Kerouac did not seem to have taken her remarks personally, however, and she smiled in the darkness at his half-serious warnings about stepping down from the Greek bed. He could be almost pleasant—and was undeniably attractive—if he would only drop the mocking tone he used when addressing her. She shrugged. It would take some time to erase the memory of their first bizarre meeting at the Boat Show.

With his qualities as a doctor, she could find no fault. His examination of Mr Jollison had been efficient, practised and thorough. Additionally, he had found the right words to settle Mrs Jollison's insecurities—Kate wished she could achieve the same professional manner, but presumably much of this ability was to do with his maturity. His briefing to her had been clear and concise. He wanted a regular monitoring of BP, pulse and temperature and had planned a diet schedule for Elena's guidance which took account of the local foods and which he required Kate to oversee. Apart from these matters, plus the normal nursing duties of ensuring the patient was clean and comfortable, her main responsibilities were to continue the exercise therapy which had been started at the Cavendish.

'About the wheelchair, Nurse.' He had regarded her with perfect seriousness. 'I take your point about its cumbersome design and it would be a simple matter for Spiro to collect a lighter weight model from me tomorrow. However, having examined the patient, I believe he now has sufficient strength to use his legs as much as possible. It would not be good for him to grow too used to artificial support. What is your opinion?'

Strangely affected by his frank and obviously sincere valuing of her advice, she hesitated somewhat, but recalling her experience and knowledge, she nodded. 'Yes, I can see that. It was only to have somewhere comfortable for him to sit, really. But I could have Spiro take one of the easy chairs out on to the verandah during the day. And he'd have his forearm crutches to hand to make him feel secure whenever he wanted to visit the bathroom.' She nodded again, slowly.

'Excellent. Also, of course, we must begin making preparations for dispensing with the crutches, *n'est-ce pas?*' He seemed pleased to have her agreement.

'Yes, we must.' She frowned. 'What we really need is a pair of parallel bars to really get him walking.' She stopped suddenly, realising he was grinning at her.

'Improvise, Nurse Trelawney. Improvise! You will find that the dining-room contains some chairs which I suspect are exactly the right design for the exercises you have in mind.'

Eventually, even the remarkable twist of fate which had caused this rather unorthodox French doctor to twice cross her path faded from her thoughts and she drifted away into a deep sleep.

CHAPTER FOUR

SHE was awake early the next morning and lay there in her new surroundings, refreshed and anticipating the day ahead. All was obviously well next door, for there had been no calls for her during the night. She stretched luxuriously, the cotton sheets smooth against her skin, and looked around the room. One of her bags lay open on a chair in the pool of early morning sunlight which slanted in through the French windows. Her clothes were in a disordered heap, spilling over the edges of her case.

She felt a satisfying sense of achievement at having arrived safely with her charges. Today would be a day for organising everything properly, establishing a pattern and getting on to the correct professional footing with Dr de Kerouac.

She pulled the bedclothes aside purposefully and put on her dressing gown and slippers. She would make a start straight away and unpack her clothes. But a shower first, she determined.

Clutching her sponge bag and towel, she quietly opened the door and made her way along the paved patio to the bathroom at the opposite end. It looked as though she were first up, for even the opposite wing, which Spiro and Elena occupied, was silent. She felt a promise of the coming day's warmth in the air and her pace quickened in anticipation of washing off the last vestige of yesterday's travel.

The bathroom was unusual, for the shower ran straight on to the sloping tiled floor, with none of the English accoutrements of curtain and base unit. How simple a warm climate made everything, she reflected. She hung her dressing gown and nightie behind the door and, standing cautiously to one side of the shower, adjusted the temperature of the water. When it was to her liking, she stepped beneath the spray with a gasp of delight. She felt the fine jets play over her body, enjoying the invigorating sensation, and then grasped her shampoo and lathered herself from top to toe.

Drying her hair in the warm morning air would not present a problem, she realised, as she briskly towelled her slim figure. She glanced down appraisingly at herself. No sign of any flabbiness after the winter, she decided. Muscles nice and trim, thanks to squash and swimming. The sleek black bikini was a definite possibility if any opportunities arose for some secluded sunbathing. Her clear skin looked and felt good with a suntan, she knew.

The villa was quiet as she returned to her room, although she fancied she heard the rattle of crockery, the sound at odds with the stillness of the morning. She decided that she still had time to explore the terraced garden before the household was fully awake. She opened the French windows, went out on to the verandah and tip-toed down some stone steps to the first terrace. It was even warmer on the south-facing side of the house and the rays of the sun were already encouraging the cicadas to start their ecstatic chirping amongst the surrounding lemon trees. The faintest beginnings of a breeze stirred her dressing-gown gently against

her bare legs. She drew in a sigh of contentment at
the idyllic scene.

The peace was suddenly disturbed by the clamour of a motor scooter, its engine being revved
hard, coming down the track on the opposite side of
the villa. A delivery of some sort, she presumed,
slightly irritated, for the noise had completely de-
stroyed the breathless quiet of the morning. She
made her way back to her room and began to
unpack.

She turned her mind to the question of what to
wear. It would be pretty oppressive to have to wear
her uniform throughout the duration of her stay,
she pondered. Perhaps a discreet word with Mrs
Jollison would be a good idea. She would continue
to change into it whenever the doctor was due to
visit, however. Somehow it seemed very important
to retain an air of formality with him. She would put
it on this morning, for it would help establish her
role in the household on the first day. As she was
about to get dressed, there was a rap at the door.

She opened it to find a complete stranger standing there. She was young, with long waving dark
hair and wearing a pair of extremely close-fitting
denim shorts, frayed at the edges and covered with
patches. A cheesecloth blouse adorned her top
half, the tails knotted across her midriff beneath
her full breasts. The thinness of the material and
the fact that she was not wearing a bra left little to
the imagination. She was tanned a deep golden
brown, from her sandalled feet to her slightly arrogant features. A pair of dark eyes surveyed Kate in
a bored manner.

'Good morning, Nurse. Dr de Kerouac asked me
to call and help you with a little elementary inter-

preting.' Something in the girl's tone caused Kate
to bristle. 'I'm sorry to have got you up.'

Kate resisted the impulse to inform this young
person that she had actually been up for almost an
hour, despite still being in her nightclothes. 'I was
just about to get dressed, Miss—?' she replied
levelly.

'Oh, everyone calls me Madeleine,' said the girl.
She tossed her head and ran a tanned hand through
her hair. 'Shall I wait for you in the kitchen?'

'By all means.' Kate peered out across the quadrangle.

'It's that door there, the second along from the
corner. I'll be with Elena and Spiro.' The girl
turned, without waiting for a reply.

Kate clicked her door shut and changed into her
uniform with all the haste of a student nurse late on
duty. She wasn't going to let this young lady convey
any criticisms of her back to Dr de Kerouac. Grabbing her notebook and pencil, she sped across the
quadrangle, her white canvas shoes crunching on
the gravel. She made for the half-open kitchen
door, through which drifted a rapid spate of Greek.

Spiro was sitting at a large, wooden table and
Madeleine was perched on its edge, one thigh lifted
and resting on the scrubbed surface, her leg dangling. They were both laughing at some shared joke,
but their merriment stilled as Kate entered, as if she
were the source of their amusement.

'Now then, Nurse, what would you like to
know?' enquired the girl.

Kate wished she had had the foresight to note
down her queries the night before. Common sense
would guide her, however. She sat down at the
table and opened her notebook.

'Well, firstly, it is important to establish regular mealtimes,' she began. 'I should like to ask what times I may expect them to be served.'

The girl turned to Spiro and delivered a quick burst of Greek. Elena's name figured largely in the exchange and Spiro half rose to his feet, presumably to fetch her. His wife forestalled him however and bustled into the kitchen from the next room, carrying a large basket of laundry.

'*Calle mera*,' she greeted Kate, smiling broadly. '*Calle mera*, Madeleine,' she added, but the smile had lost some of its warmth, replaced by an expression of mild disapproval as she observed the girl lounging on the table. She thumped the basket of laundry down next to Madeleine, who casually slid both legs to the ground and pulled up a kitchen chair, which she reversed and sat on, her elbows resting on its backrest and legs splayed out to either side. If anything, the look of disapproval on Elena's face deepened.

The torrent of Greek resumed, this time with contributions from Elena. Heavens, thought Kate. If a simple request to be given mealtimes was this complicated, they would be sitting in the kitchen all morning. Eventually, however, Madeleine raised a hand and turned to Kate. 'Nine a.m., one p.m., and supper at seven p.m. OK? Elena is also very proud of her ability to serve English tea and will make some every afternoon at about four, if everybody wishes it. And coffee at eleven in the morning. Yes?'

'That sounds fine,' replied Kate. Then, realising that Elena and Spiro were looking at her anxiously awaiting a reply, she smiled at them and said 'OK', nodding vigorously.

Relief reigned, with Spiro and Elena repeating 'OK' at each other. Spiro got up to go.

'There are a couple of other things,' said Kate hurriedly and he disappointedly sat down again as Madeleine translated.

'There's the question of Mr Jollison's diet . . .'

But from then on, things went remarkably simply. The diet sheet left by the doctor for Elena's guidance turned out to have English translations already thoughtfully provided and, in a very short space of time, Kate had obtained answers for most of the domestic matters which had been concerning her.

'Well, if that's all for the moment, I must be going,' said Madeleine, rising to her feet. 'I've a yacht charter to check in at ten o'clock.'

Kate smiled her thanks at Elena as the two girls made their way out of the kitchen.

'Where do you work?' she asked Madeleine politely.

'At Ionian Yacht Charters near Kalami, a mile or two up the coast. Although you can't call it work. I'm a sort of Girl Friday.' The bored tone had returned to her voice. 'Spiro works there part-time too, does the odd bit of maintenance two or three mornings a week. I mean, there's not enough to keep him busy here, is there? Anyway, if you're OK, I'll see you. Day after tomorrow, I suppose, about the same time.'

They had reached the girl's battered motor scooter.

'Well, I'm very grateful, Madeleine. It's very kind of you to spare the time. I'll soon get organised. I feel a bit silly, really, not speaking the language.'

The girl maintained a non-committal silence and made to lift her scooter off its stand. She paused and clicked open the glove compartment. 'Dr de Kerouac asked me to get you one of these.' She thrust a booklet at Kate. 'You'll probably find it useful.'

Kate looked down at the title 'Useful Phrases in Greek,' it read. A tourist handbook indeed! She felt a wave of indignation and sought a suitably cool reply, but Madeleine had kicked her machine into life and was roaring out of the gate, a hand lifted carelessly in farewell. Kate was left standing in the courtyard, feeling rather foolish and not a little resentful.

She banished these thoughts and turned her attention to the morning's tasks. If breakfast was to be at nine, she just had sufficient time before it was served to get through the routine of BP, temperature and pulse readings and make sure her patient was washed and comfortable. She had arranged for meals to continue to be served in the Jollisons' room, at least until he was mobile enough to sit in the dining-room.

After breakfast, she managed to communicate to Spiro that she wanted one of the easy chairs moved out to the verandah. She settled Paul Jollison down with a book and an ample supply of cushions.

'Don't get too comfortable, mind,' she said, tucking a blanket round his legs. 'I'm going to make sure you do some work this morning, after coffee.'

'What did you have in mind, dear?' enquired Mary Jollison as Kate went back into their room to straighten his bed.

'The doctor and I want to get him making more use of his leg,' she said quietly. 'I have some exercises in mind, using chairs. I'm just going off to work them out. We don't want him getting too dependent on wheelchairs and crutches, you see.'

'It's not too soon, then?' asked Mary Jollison anxiously.

'Not at all, Mrs Jollison. Dr de Kerouac and I do understand these things, you know.'

'Yes dear. Of course. I'm sorry to be such a worrier.'

'That's all right, it's natural.' She paused. 'Although I do think it would be better if Mr Jollison and I did his exercises without you being present,' she said firmly. 'He'll be able to concentrate better.' Sensing that this might have sounded a little unkind, she added, 'Why don't you explore the garden? Actually, there's a gate in the wall at the bottom. I expect it leads down to the sea.'

Leaving Mrs Jollison suitably diverted, she sought out the dining-room and the chairs which the doctor had suggested she improvise with. He had practically issued a challenge, she decided, certainly one she would respond to.

For many patients the ability to stand upright is a great morale booster and generally regarded as a milestone of progress. However, there was little point in Paul Jollison's ability to stand upright, or even walk, unless he were able to do so unaided, his greatest difficulty being to rise to a standing position without help. At present he was very reliant on either his crutches or a supporting arm from Kate. It was important to get him a stage further on from that.

She stood in the cool, shuttered dining-room and assessed whether the stability and height of the chairs would provide a suitable means to this end.

She decided they would and, again with Spiro's help—it was apparently a morning when he was not occupied with his part-time job—three of them were carried through to the Jollisons' room.

By lunchtime, she pronounced much satisfaction with their progress. After a few false starts, she managed to arrange him with his feet as close to the chair as possible and sufficiently widely spaced to provide an effective base of support for his body. The backs of the remaining chairs acted as a pair of rails on which he could pull himself up. She started by placing a hand on the crown of his head and asking him to push against it in order to provide a focus of attention for aligning his muscles. After several tries, he was managing well without her help.

'That's very good, Mr Jollison. The next stage is for you to push up with your hands on the seat of the chair, rather than pull down from the backs of the others. You're doing jolly well, though.'

He sighed. 'One certainly takes a lot for granted. You never think about sitting and standing normally. I never realised how complicated it all was.'

'It'll seem simpler with each passing day,' she said. 'But we've got to take it a little at a time.'

'Yes, I'm sure you're right, Kate, but I'm the impatient sort. I was sitting looking at those lemon trees over the wall, all covered in blossom. Have you ever smelled a crushed lemon leaf?'

She shook her head, smiling.

'It's quite something, I can tell you. I'm really looking forward to the day I can get down through that garden and do some exploring for myself.'

'It won't be long,' promised Kate. 'But for the moment, it's time for lunch and then a quiet nap.'

Whether it was the effect of the lunch, or the midday warmth, or indeed a combination of both, the short siesta she had prescribed for her patient seemed an irresistible idea and she indulged herself with a short sleep.

By the time the doctor was due to visit, however, she was bright and wide awake, one ear listening for the sound of his car.

He arrived brusque and efficient and it was clear he was adopting a distant manner today. She felt a slight sense of relief and stood attentively on the opposite side of the bed, whilst he examined Jollison and ran an eye over the charted general observations she had been compiling. She thought he seemed pleased as their patient described the exercise routine she had instigated. After his examination they walked leisurely back to his car.

'Well, you seem to have things pretty well under control here, Nurse. He's doing fine. His reflexes aren't quite back to normal, though. Not surprising really, with the blow on the head he suffered and the skull fracture. We still need to keep a close watch on him.'

She nodded.

'You were able to make use of the chairs then?' He was smiling at her.

'Yes, I was. It's surprising what you can do with simple equipment, isn't it?'

'It certainly is. It irritates me, when I think how pampered we are with the medical services in our own countries. The communities here do not have anything like it.' His expression had hardened. 'I don't really approve of private medicine, you know.'

She felt she was somehow included in this sweeping statement and felt compelled to make a mild retort. 'But Mr Jollison's a private patient.'

'That's different. It enables me to subsidise my treatment of the less well-off. Believe me, I had my fill of private medicine in Paris—the bourgeoisie, with their imagined ailments and delicate constitutions. And London's no different.' He was glaring into the distance, his jaw set.

Perhaps he included the Cavendish Square Clinic in this condemnation. She wanted to protest that her sojourn at the clinic was just a mild easing of the pace after the Intensive Care Unit at South Devon General, a convenient stepping-stone into London. She fully intended to go back to more basic nursing as soon as she felt able. But she was tongue-tied and a little confused by his unexpected outburst.

He opened the door of the Alfa-Romeo and deposited his bag on the back seat.

She found a welcome change of subject. 'Oh, thank you for asking Madeleine to call by. She was a great help.'

'*Bon.* I thought she would be.'

'Of course, the phrase book will be invaluable.' She realised she had barely disguised the underlying note of irony in her voice and added, 'Madeleine is quite a . . .' She hesitated.

'Lively girl? *Certainement.*' He was grinning.

'You know her well, then?' She had asked the question before she realised it was in her mind.

'You could say that.' His long frame folded smoothly as he slid down behind the wheel of the low-slung car. 'Well, *au revoir*, Nurse. I will come again tomorrow at the same time, but then on alternate days after that, I think.'

She nodded in agreement. Then he was reversing

the car, ready to pull out of the courtyard and she turned to go back indoors.

'Oh, Nurse.' He had stopped and was beckoning her towards the car again. She walked over as he flicked the gear lever back into neutral and looked up at her, a tanned dark-haired arm resting on the edge of the door frame.

'It occurs to me that a young lady like you should be able to enjoy the occasional evening off. Some friends of mine, an English couple, are having a few people round for drinks and supper tomorrow evening. Would you care to come? I could arrange for you to be invited.'

'That would be lovely,' she replied eagerly. 'But what about—?'

'I think the Jollisons could be left for a few hours, there is a telephone where we are going,' he said. 'My friends' villa is in Kalami—we could make our way there after my visit late tomorrow afternoon. You would like that?'

'Well yes, I would, if you're sure.' She was slightly surprised at the enthusiasm of her own response and dropped her eyes from his gaze. '*Alors, à demain,*' he said—and was gone in a crackle of exhaust.

By the following afternoon, Kate was really looking forward to an evening out. The Jollisons had settled in well and she had no qualms about leaving them. She had mentioned the possibility of her little excursion to Mrs Jollison over lunch.

'Only if Doctor's happy with Mr Jollison of course—there's a 'phone where we're going,' she went on.

'I'm sure that will be fine, my dear,' replied Mrs

Jollison. 'It will do you good to get out and meet some different people. You don't want to be cooped up all the time, with just Paul and me for company. Have you got something pretty to wear?'

'I was going to have a look through my things while Mr Jollison was having his after lunch sleep.' She hesitated for a moment. 'Actually, I was going to ask if you and Mr Jollison minded if I were a little less formal occasionally.' Mrs Jollison looked puzzled. 'That is,' went on Kate, 'perhaps I could dress more casually, not always be in uniform I mean.'

The expression on Mrs Jollison's face cleared. 'My dear! Of course you can. You don't want to be prim and proper all the time, especially as the weather gets warmer. Why don't you and I make it a rule always to dress for dinner in the evening. That would be nice, wouldn't it? But as for the rest of the day, why not wear what you like? Paul doesn't stand on ceremony and anyway, you're a very good nurse and I'm very relieved you're with us. It doesn't matter a jot what you wear.'

'Oh, I think I should be in uniform whenever the doctor's due to visit,' added Kate, 'but the rest of the time, it would be lovely to relax a little. Thank you.'

Mrs Jollison was waving her hand in the air, banishing Kate's gratitude. 'It's nothing, my dear, nothing at all. But you must promise me one thing in return.'

'Of course,' replied Kate. 'What is it?'

'You must drop the "Mr" and "Mrs" and start calling us Paul and Mary.'

Kate hesitated and then, anxious not to offend Mrs Jollison, answered, 'I'd like to do that, er

Mary, but the doctor might not approve. He seems to have very fixed ideas about etiquette and . . .'

'Well, why don't we keep the "Mr and Mrs"— and the uniform—just for his visits? I agree that he is the sort of man with whom things should be kept as formal as possible.'

Kate realised that Mary Jollison appeared to be twinkling at her for some reason.

Looking through her wardrobe later on, she realised that on this occasion she would have to break her self-made rule about being in uniform whenever he came. He had said they were to leave after his visit and he would not want to be kept waiting while she changed. In the end, she selected a light blue cotton jersey dress as providing the right degree of formality for the evening. It had the advantage of also being warm, for she had noticed that the evenings felt quite chill after the sun's heat had gone. She would take her dark blue velvet jacket as well, for the same reason. A pair of slingback high heels and her suede pochette bag completed the outfit.

She surveyed the finished result in the full length mirror in her room. She certainly looked smart enough, she decided. The jersey dress, with its belt at the waist, was flattering to the gentle contours of her figure and the colours were an effective combination with her grey eyes and fair hair. She leaned forward for a final check on make-up. Never a girl to use a great deal of it, she reflected on how nice it would be to develop a suntan. Then she could even dispense with the slight touch of blusher which she normally wore. She was really looking forward to seeing some new faces, together with the short excursion up the coast. She felt she had successfully settled everyone in at the Villa Netriti and it would be nice to explore beyond its boundaries.

She gave a start as she heard the distinctive note of the Alfa Romeo coming down the track. He was early this evening. She breathed a sigh of relief that she had left herself plenty of time to shower and dress, and flew next door to make sure the bed was neat and the patient ready. She plumped the pillows and straightened the coverlet, smiling acknowledgement at the Jollisons' compliments on her attire.

'Quite charming, my dear,' beamed Mary. 'I hope you have a lovely time.'

The doctor's reaction was nowhere near as warm. He inspected her with what appeared to be blank disapproval and she felt relieved that the bed—and his waiting patient—was between them.

'I thought you wouldn't want to delay while I changed, so I got ready in advance,' she blurted, somewhat at a loss as to why she felt so compelled to offer an explanation.

His eyebrow arched sardonically. 'Of course,' he murmured. 'Quite a transformation.' He dumped his bag on the bed and fished in it for his stethoscope. Kate busied herself making a totally unnecessary examination of the temperature and pulse charts. Somehow, her anticipation and sense of pleasure at the evening ahead had evaporated. She retreated into monosyllabic replies to his routine questions.

'*Enfin,*' he announced, snapping his bag shut. 'Another day of good progress, I would say. And now, Mr Jollison, would you say Nurse Trelawney has earned an evening off? She has obviously prepared for one.'

'But of course,' replied Paul Jollison and grinned at her. She returned his smile, although inwardly she was fuming—and within an inch of informing this supercilious Frenchman what he could do with his evening. But he had launched into reassurances that they would be just fifteen minutes drive away, that he would brief Spiro to telephone if the Jollisons had a moment's concern and she withdrew to her room to collect her bag and jacket. She was determined not to let him spoil things. A slightly distant, uncaring manner was her best defence. She should have made him wait while she changed, she thought angrily, as she heard him leave the Jollison's room. She shut her door behind her to see him waiting by the car. His eyes appraised her as she made her way across the quadrangle.

He opened the passenger door with a flourish and, summoning her maximum dignity, she smoothly settled into the seat, swinging her legs in after her.

'You will find an adjustment lever beneath your knees if you wish more leg room,' he said. 'I will just go and instruct Spiro and then we can go.' He pushed the door shut.

What a creature of changing moods he was, she reflected, as she settled herself in her seat. One minute frowning disapproval, the next dancing attention.

His feet crunched on the gravel and he slid lithely in beside her.

'Seat-belts, I think,' he said. 'Here . . .' He reached across her shoulder as she looked for the buckle. 'And here, so. It is comfortable, yes?' He paused, looking for a reply, and she nodded.

'I was a little early. It was thoughtful of you to be ready.' Kate almost gaped, but he had not noticed her amazement, for he was flicking the engine into life, concentrating on reversing out of the courtyard. He selected first gear and looked at her again.

'We will arrive and I will introduce you to my friends. I am sure you will like them. Then unfortunately I have to make a quick house call. It is a Greek woman in Kalami, expecting her eighth child—these Greeks, they are, how can I say? Prolific?' He was laughing and she found herself responding. 'Anyway, she has slight blood pressure and is well into her thirties. I like to keep an eye on her. The visit will take only a short while, but I will make sure you are looked after while I am absent. You do not mind?'

'Of course not,' she replied. 'I could come with you if you need any help.'

'Thank you, but that will not be necessary. It is only the fifth month of her pregnancy. A routine visit really.'

He revved the engine and they accelerated up the rough track. He drove with sensitivity, for the sleek lines and cockpit-like feel of the Alfa Romeo's interior suggested a great deal of power. The suspension jumped and bucked as they climbed away from the villa, the steering-wheel dancing in his hand. But she had no impression of the unnecessary ostentatiousness normally associated with drivers of red sports cars.

They reached the main road and he accelerated away in the direction signposted Kalami, the burble of the Alfa's exhaust rising into a crackle. He drove with speed, not haste, and she leaned back, enjoying the pace.

'Also,' he added, smoothly easing the stub gear lever into fifth gear and quieting the engine's roar, 'being early means it is still daylight and you will be able to see more of Corfu.'

She smiled acknowledgement and he returned to concentrating on his driving.

The road climbed and twisted in and out of groves of lemon and olive trees and now and again they passed through small villages. The heat had gone from the day and the local inhabitants were going about their business. There were frequent occasions when they reduced speed to overtake people riding donkeys—or leading them, the patient beasts carrying seemingly impossible loads, their heads swinging rhythmically from side to side as they plodded along.

An assortment of smells were borne in through the open windows of the car, the elusive scents of blossom and foliage and, in the villages, the tantalising aromas of evening meals being cooked. Kate realised that she was looking forward to supper very much.

She was immediately made to feel welcome by their hosts. Their home was as delightful as the Villa Netriti, but in a different, more modern style. It boasted a swimming pool, for example, with a splendid brick barbecue at one end of its tiled surround, where their host was busy coaxing a bed of charcoal into life. He and the doctor were obviously old friends and he turned to Kate with a smile of pleasure.

'How very pleasant to meet you, Miss Trelawney. I am delighted that Laurent has allowed you to take a little time off. I bet he is a hard taskmaster?'

She found herself shaking hands with a pleasant-faced Englishman called Giles Stephens.

'As matter of fact, it is a change to see the hard working doctor relaxing a little, eh Laurent? Normally I only see him get his mind off his work when he is at the helm of that yacht of his.'

'Perhaps so,' said the doctor with a shrug. 'Now, I fear you will think me ungracious, for I have to leave your party for a while to visit a patient in Kalami.'

'You see?' Giles was looking at Kate in mock exasperation. 'And Miss Trelawney here? You're going to desert her, as soon as she has arrived? Shame on you, Laurent.'

'Come now, Giles, I have already asked Miss Trelawney if she objects and she does not. I am sure you will look after her while I am gone.'

'It will be a pleasure. We will leave this ungallant Frenchman, Miss Trelawney, and I will introduce you to some far more interesting people, who will be delighted to have your company. But first a glass of wine.'

Before she could object, Giles had taken her arm and dismissing the doctor with a mock-serious wave of his hand, steered her towards a long table on which were laid out wine glasses and an array of interesting looking food.

'Now then, Kate, you would like some white wine? It is nicely chilled and will go well with my wife's sea-food hors d'oeuvres—it's one of her specialities.' He poured her a glass and replenished his own.

'Do you often go sailing with Dr Kerouac?' asked Kate.

'Quite often—although it's rather a busman's holiday. Jean and I run Ionian Yacht Charters you see, and we have quite enough of boats as it is. But Laurent is good company and he has a beautiful boat—a *Nautor Swan*.'

'Of course,' said Kate. She remembered he had actually been in the process of buying the yacht when she had so embarrassingly fallen into it at the Boat Show. 'I believe I've seen it,' she added vaguely.

'Yes, he keeps her moored in a bay by the road you came along.'

Somehow Kate refrained from describing the *true* occasion when she had first seen the *Swan*—on dry land at Earls Court. It seemed a rather complicated, inappropriate sort of story. She smiled non-committally.

'Do you like boats yourself, Kate,' enquired Giles.

'Oh yes. I've done quite a bit of sailing at home, down in the West Country. My father was in the Navy.'

'Was he indeed? Well, you must tell Laurent. He sometimes allows himself the luxury of a crew,' laughed Giles. 'Bit of a loner though, really. He sailed that yacht single-handed from Monte Carlo last month. February it was, and still a chance of winter storms.'

'But that must be well over a thousand sea miles,' said Kate in astonishment.

'Yes, it is. But Laurent is a very good seaman, like many Frenchmen. I have often tried to persuade him to give up his medical practice and come in as a partner in my charter company, but he is dedicated to his profession.'

'Has he always practised in Corfu?'

'Oh good heavens, no. He fled here from Paris. Had to get away from all those hypochondriacs, he claims, but I think there was something else. *Cherchez la femme*, I think. He's an attractive fellow.'

They were interrupted by a pretty, dark-haired woman taking Giles's arm.

'*There* you are, darling. You'll have to go and get the barbecue sizzling. I think we're almost a full house and people are beginning to nibble at things on the table.' She turned to Kate. 'Hallo, I'm Jean Stephens, Giles's wife.'

Giles excused himself and after introducing Kate to his wife, withdrew to his responsibilities as chef. 'She likes sailing, Jean. Find her some people she'd enjoy talking boats with.' He disappeared into the not inconsiderable throng which had now gathered.

Jean steered Kate into a group of mixed nationalities, all thankfully speaking English, where she was warmly welcomed, with much friendly interest expressed in her reasons for being in Corfu. The time passed and she began to enjoy herself enormously. Jean was an excellent hostess and contrived to keep glasses filled, food circulated and people mingling. The time passed quickly.

Eventually, she found herself chatting with a rather suave Greek. It transpired that he was a local architect.

'As a matter of fact, this property was one of my projects.' He waved airily around him. 'It is good, yes?'

'Yes, it is very beautiful,' she agreed and then politely added, 'It must be difficult to build on such a steep hill-side.'

'Ah, I see you appreciate these things,' said her companion grandly. 'That is in order to take advantage of the view across the bay.' His eyes flickered over her. 'Come, I will show you.'

Before she could protest, he had taken her arm and was steering her away from the knot of people clustered around the swimming pool. He was very overpowering and wore an extremely obvious eau de cologne. However, it would be impolite to protest and it was a genuine interest she had expressed in the villa.

They reached the opposite side of the building and she saw that they were on a balcony looking out over the sea.

'There, you see. A magnificent view.'

Kate nodded, for the truth of his observation was obvious. Her eyes were not yet completely accustomed to the darkness, but she could see that the scene was quite breathtaking. The moon had risen and was reflected in a line of ripples which extended from their vantage point out to the horizon. She could hear the gentle wash of waves breaking on the rocks below.

'And over there, just tucked inside the headland, are the yacht moorings. Your Villa Netriti is just round the point.'

She peered into the darkness but could not really distinguish anything.

'Here, you are looking the wrong way.' He had moved behind her and was placing a hand on either side of her head and turning her gaze to the right. His face seemed unnecessarily close to hers as he sighted along her angle of view. Finding his proximity, with the smell of his cologne, most unwelcome, she hurriedly nodded and made to step away.

'I see that you have been well looked after during my absence. Nurse Trelawney.' A voice edged with sarcasm intruded on her consciousness.

She turned and, slightly relieved, saw the doctor standing there. She had not heard him come round the corner of the villa and could not make out his face in the darkness.

'Oh yes. I was just admiring the house. It was designed by Mr er . . .' She trailed off, realising her companion's unfamiliar Greek name was beyond her.

'Mr Dimitros, Stephan Dimitros,' the doctor finished the sentence for her. 'But surely you have been introduced?' The edge in his voice was now very noticeable.

'Of course we have—it's just the pronunciation. I find it difficult,' she retorted, puzzled by his tone. 'It is quite an achievement to build such a beautiful house on such a difficult site.'

'Yes. Mr Dimitros has *many* achievements to his credit, *n'est-ce pas*, Stephan?'

'*Mais oui*, Laurent,' replied the Greek. She had a fleeting sensation that they were sharing some secret joke at her expense.

'I think I'll rejoin the party,' she announced. 'Thank you for showing me the villa.' She made her way back to the pool, the two men following. Realising that the glass she was carrying was empty, she turned back to them.

'I would quite like another glass of wine. May I bring you both one as well?'

'Regrettably, it is time I left,' replied Dimitros. 'You will forgive me. Goodbye, Miss Trelawney, it has been a pleasure.' He took her hand and lightly

brushed it with his lips. She withdrew her arm
swiftly, aware of the doctor's eye upon her.

'Goodbye Mr Di—Dimitros,' she attempted
clumsily and was rather glad to watch him make his
way over to their hosts to bid his farewells.

'I am surprised that you feel able to take another
glass of wine, Nurse,' the doctor's comment was
sardonic.

'What on earth do you mean?' she enquired
hotly.

'Oh come now, *ma petite mademoiselle*. You
obviously do not have the head for it.'

'Are you suggesting I'm—?' she cried in amazement, unable to frame the question properly in her
indignation.

He stared down at her condescendingly. 'It is
your normal practice to encourage advances from
complete strangers, then?'

'Certainly not,' she hissed, infuriated not only by
his suggestion, but also at being inhibited in her
anger by the press of people surrounding them.
'And he was *not* making a pass at me!'

'Oh I see. A moonlit scene on a balcony over-
looking the sea,' he scoffed. 'Stephan Dimitros is
one of the worst philanderers I have ever met. He
seems to have a particularly telling effect on a
certain type of young English girl—particularly
tourists.' He took the glass from her hand and went
over to Giles, who was making his way through the
throng, carrying a bottle of wine. She remained
rooted to the spot, mouth agape at his effron-
tery.

Miserably wishing she was able to make her way
home on her own, she was obliged to spend the
remainder of the evening standing helplessly at his

elbow while he made light conversation with his friends. He seemed to be excluding her from this small talk with studied deliberation and by the time the party began to break up, she was close to tears of humiliation. However, she summoned enough composure to thank Giles and Jean for their hospitality.

'You must come and visit us again—that is, if this tyrant will allow you a respite from your duties,' smiled Giles. 'Perhaps the four of us could have a day or two's cruising in that *Swan* of yours, Laurent.'

The need for them to respond to this suggestion was negated by a further group of leave-takers, anxious to thank their hosts, and she followed him out to the car.

The journey back to the Villa Netriti passed in an icy silence. He drove at speed, the tyres protesting on the bends, and her sidelong glance revealed a set expression on his face and pursed lips, lit by the glow of the instrument panel lights.

As the car crunched to a halt on the gravel of the villa courtyard, she forestalled any courtesy he may have intended in opening her door and was out of the car and round to the driver's side almost before he himself could emerge.

Summoning every ounce of composure, she drew in a breath and glared up at his face. 'I should like to thank you for asking me to accompany you this evening. *Parts* of it have been quite enjoyable. I should also like to repeat that I am not in the habit of inviting passes from complete strangers, least of all from over-perfumed Greeks. I imagine we will next meet when you call on Mr Jollison again. The day after tomorrow?' She looked at him, trying to match the lack of concern in her voice with a suitably cold expression.

Suddenly, to her utter amazement, he had stepped forward and pulled her roughly towards him with an arm on each of her shoulders. Her mouth parted in a gasp as his lips closed over hers. The force of his movement caused her to step back and, feeling insecure on the shifting gravel, she groped for support, her hands closing blindly on his waist. Somehow this gesture seemed to get mixed up with everything else. Against her every rational wish she found herself responding to his lips, her arms tightening around him. She closed her eyes.

His mouth left hers and traced a path of exquisite sensation across the contours of her face. She tilted her head back and saw the dark canopy of the sky, alive with its trillion stars, as if in a dream.

'*Voici une petite leçon d'amour, ma chère Anglaise*,' he breathed in her ear. She could sense an urgency in him and felt a delicious languor beginning to steal over her.

'*Et encore une fois*,' he murmured and his lips returned to hers. He was holding her very tightly now and she knew he could feel the soft firmness of her breasts straining against his chest as she lifted an arm to let her fingers caress the crinkly hair at the nape of his neck.

Then his earlier mood seemed to reassert itself and as suddenly as he had caught her he released her. She stood swaying slightly as he folded his long frame back into the Alfa.

'*D'accord*, mademoiselle. Until the day after tomorrow.' He engaged the gears with a crunch and was gone in a spurt of gravel and a blaze of headlights sweeping over the silent cypress trees.

She stood in the courtyard as quiet returned to the darkened villa, her senses reeling from the intensity of his embrace and the abruptness of his departure.

CHAPTER FIVE

THE days passed and began to merge into weeks. Following the events in the courtyard, Kate had prepared with some trepidation for the doctor's next visit, feeling quite sure she would be unable to look him in the eye. But he had adopted an air of polite detachment and swiftly dealt with the routine of his examination. He maintained this demeanour on subsequent calls.

To her surprise, she found she mildly resented this apparent erasing of the memory of their encounter. It seemed that he had felt no inhibitions about making the sort of casual advance which he had earlier so unjustly accused her of encouraging from that Greek. He was obviously a man of double standards. Yet his actions had seemed far from casual, and, now and again, often in those half-awake moments in the mornings which precede full consciousness, she found her mind returning to the memory of strong fingers gripping her shoulders and firm lips on hers. She would refuse to dwell on these recollections, however, and would despatch them with an angry shrug and throw herself into the day's activities.

The exercise therapy began to greatly improve Paul Jollison's mobility and the day arrived when he negotiated the entire length of the verandah with only the aid of a walking stick. With much ceremony she bore the now redundant crutches aloft and out of the room to be placed in a store cupboard.

'It looks as though you'll soon have no need of me,' she remarked to Mary later that day as they sat enjoying their after-lunch coffee.

'Nonsense, Kate,' cried Mary. 'We are both very relieved to have you with us, myself particularly. Paul still has his vague moments and once or twice I've caught him looking at me as though I were a complete stranger.' She paused, concern furrowing her forehead. 'It's very worrying.'

'No it's not, Mary.' Kate leaned forward to pat her companion's hand. 'It will take a long time for him to completely get over the severe head injury he experienced. We can't hurry things.' She smiled wryly. 'But he doesn't need nearly as much nursing as when we first arrived.'

'Well then, my dear,' exclaimed Mary, 'you've earned a little time to yourself. Why don't you take the afternoon off. It is Saturday after all. Do some exploring. That path at the bottom of the garden does lead down to the sea, you know.'

'Yes, I believe it does. I've been part of the way but never had time to follow it right down.'

'Off you go then,' urged Mary. 'Paul and I will be perfectly all right and the break will be good for you.'

'Well, it would be lovely,' she replied uncertainly. 'If you're really sure . . . ?'

'Of course, my dear. Why don't you take your swimming things? The days are really warm now and you could do a little sunbathing. You'll look lovely with a tan.'

Needing no further encouragement, Kate rose to her feet and sped to her room to collect some

things. Suntan cream, sunglasses and a towel flew
into her raffia shoulder bag. After a moment's
speculation, the skimpy black bikini followed.
There might well be a secluded little sunbathing
spot along the way, she mused, even if she were
unable to find a beach. The denim skirt and short
sleeved cotton blouse she was already wearing were
perfect for clambering down rough paths—as were
her flat leather sandals.

With a lighthearted 'See you later' to Mary, she
skipped nimbly down the stone steps to the terraced garden, exulting in the warm play of the
afternoon sun on her bare arms. She felt a pleasant
sense of anticipation as she pushed open the rickety
wooden gate in the moss-covered wall and made
her way into the lemon grove. The perfume from
the trees' blossom was almost overpowering. As
she moved away from the villa, the full heat of the
day assailed her. She slowed her brisk pace down to
an easy dawdle.

The flat rocky ground reflected the waves of
shimmering heat back up at her and she was glad to
feel a gentle sea breeze on her face as she emerged
from the trees to find that the path forked.

In one direction, to her left, it ran along the high
level northwards, in the direction of Kalami. The
other fork led down, presumably towards the sea.
Taking this latter route, she discovered it began to
zig-zag and drop quite sharply and she could soon
see a tiny inlet not far below, into which the gentle
Mediterranean swell lapped. It was completely deserted.

Picking her way with care, she negotiated the
descent. Here and there the occasional step had
been roughly hewn out of the rock, but there were

no handholds and she was glad to be sensibly
dressed.

She reached the bottom and kicked off her sandals. Dangling them from one hand, she stepped
down to the water. With indrawn breath she ventured ankle deep into its crystal clarity. She stood
there, drinking in the scene, the coolness of the sea
a delicious refreshment. It would be absolutely
heavenly to go for a swim. It was a pity that the little
cove was in shade, for the ancient cliffs rising above
her just obscured the sun, still fairly low in its spring
sky. Her eyes surveyed the run of the southfacing
shoreline as it swung away out to the Kalami headland. Tumbled piles of flat rocks lay along the base
of the cliffs. They were basking in full sunshine a
short distance from where she stood, where the
inlet widened out to the azure blue sea.

Nothing ventured, nothing gained, she resolved
and, lifting the hem of the denim skirt, she waded
to a convenient climbing-out place which gave
access to the rocks. She began picking her way
carefully over the craggy terrain. Within a short
while she had emerged into full sunlight again and
to her delight came upon an especially large, flat-
surfaced slab. Although it was set back amongst the
others, it was lying at such an angle as to provide a
gently shelving slope down into the water. It was as
though she had come upon a secret place—apart
from a narrow angle open to the sea, a completely
secluded, private pool.

She deposited her bag on the rock, the prospect
of a cooling swim even more appealing after the
strenuous clamber over the rocks.

No need for complicated changing procedures
either, she thought, delving for her bikini. There

was even an overhang above her which shielded the
spot from any casual observers on the cliff top. She
swiftly exchanged panties for bikini bottom, slipped out of skirt and cotton blouse and reached
behind to unclip her bra. She bent down for the
bikini top but paused, struck by a rather attractive
notion, for the caress of the gentle breeze on her
bare skin was almost sensual, the sense of freedom
a delight. She looked around her surroundings
again and with sudden resolve pushed the bikini top
back into her beach bag. She had never been
swimming topless in her adult life and here was an
ideal opportunity.

She covered the short distance to the water's
edge and plunged in. It was cold, for the sea had
still to reach its summer temperature. But the
exhilarating sluice of water across her body and the
liberated sensation of her bare breasts made her
gasp with pleasure. She splashed away from the
shore in a fast over-arm, raising the water in cres-
cents of glittering droplets. Beneath her the shelving rocks dropped away into an underwater
canyon, full of wafting seaplants and darting fish.

She paused, breathless, and turning on to her
back, lay face up, floating on the softly undulating
swell. She breathed a sigh of deep contentment.
Who said there were no fringe benefits in nursing?
She lay there for a while, keeping afloat with occasional strokes of her arms. Eventually the slight
chill of the water began to penetrate and she lazily
swam back. She seized her towel and briskly dried
herself. Then she applied liberal amounts of suntan
cream to her front, spread out her towel and lay
back on the warm rock.

Gradually the heat of the sun began to seep into

her body, producing a delicious languor. This was a far cry from the uncertainties of the English April weather, she reflected. She could hardly wish for anything more—a very easy to care for patient, to whose progress she knew she was contributing, beautiful surroundings and the chance to do a little sunbathing as well. She might even be able to come here for a swim every day, while the Jollisons took their afternoon siesta. It was so peaceful. There was nothing, not even the cry of a sea bird to disturb the quiet of the silent rocks, sleeping in the warmth of the afternoon. Even the frenzied chirping of the cicadas was noticeable by its absence. The only sound was the gentle lapping of the wavelets on the rocks.

A long, low whistle penetrated her consciousness. She must have dozed off. For a split second she was completely at a loss to recognise her surroundings. She frowned, trying to collect her thoughts as the sound came again. Suddenly she remembered where she was and sat up abruptly. A lean brown figure on a wind surfer was just disappearing from view behind a rocky outcrop. An arm was raised in greeting.

'Formidable!'

The word travelled easily across the embarrassingly short distance which separated them. Kate's arm flew across her breasts to cover herself. Even though he had disappeared from her view, she felt the colour rising hotly to her cheeks.

Then, to her consternation she saw the bow of the wind surfer reappearing. The infuriating Frenchman had turned round and was sailing past again! With an undignified scramble she knelt up and, grabbing the towel, covered her nakedness.

She glared across at him. The flash of his teeth against the dark tan of his skin was very visible. Heaven knew how long he had been observing her while she had dozed. Her cheeks burned.

'I was on my way to pay a social visit to the villa,' he called. 'But it seems I have come at an inconvenient moment for you?' He was grinning at her, like some adolescent.

'I'm sure the Jollisons will be delighted to see you,' she muttered. He had brought the sailboard up into wind and stopped. She had to grudgingly admire his skill. He cupped a hand to his ear in an exaggerated gesture.

'Comment?'

'I'm sure the Jollisons will be delighted to see you,' she repeated. Heavens, she was practically shouting. She dropped her eyes, anger and embarrassment mingling.

'But you are not so delighted to see me, I think?'

She looked up again, but the words of protest stilled in her throat. He was leaning back on the surfer, his legs flexing to counterbalance the sail and with an effortless surge, caught a puff of wind and vanished from view on his original course.

Despite her relief at his disappearance, the spell of solitude was completely broken and she groped for her bra and blouse, unaware that she was still ridiculously clutching the towel to her bosom. She dressed hurriedly.

Where on earth had he come from? The shore had seemed completely deserted and she had not seen any suitable launching points for a wind surfer. Still smarting with resentment, she gathered together her things. The pleasure of the afternoon had completely evaporated. It was not even as if she made a habit of being so uninhibited. It had been such a delightful feeling of freedom to lie in the sun wearing just the minimum. It had only been the privacy suggested by this beautiful place which had encouraged her. And of all people to compromise her, it would just have to be him, she thought furiously. Any considerate man would have passed on by, chivalrously allowing her to imagine she had been unobserved. He had behaved like some cheap voyeur. She began making her way back along the rocks.

By the time she had reached the little sandy inlet and the path back up the cliffs, she had regained some of her composure. Even the sight of the wind surfer drawn up on the beach like some stranded sea creature caused only mild qualms. It seemed that he had continued in his intention to call at the villa. Her sense of outrage had given way to indifference and she was quite certain that she would be able to greet him coolly. She began to clamber up the winding path.

As she climbed, she was aware of a slight soreness on her shoulders. Despite the filter cream she had caught the sun slightly. She must have slept for quite a while.

A little out of breath, she reached the cliff top and made her way through the lemon grove. As she reached the garden of the villa she could hear voices raised in animated conversation. She could make out Mary's, which seemed to carry a great deal of consternation, but it was impossible to make out what she was saying through voluble bursts of Greek from Elena. A male voice was in the background, attempting to reassure. She quickened her pace.

She stepped up on to the verandah and met the doctor emerging from the Jollisons' room. He was wearing a pair of dark blue swimming shorts, a towelling parka and a pair of leather sandals. He stepped back and leaned a nonchalant arm against the door frame, crossing one tanned leg over the other. He eyed her scornfully.

'So. You are to grace us with your presence after all.' The note of sarcasm in his voice was dominant.

'I beg your pardon?' she replied coldly.

'Ah, but it is Mrs Jollison's pardon you should be begging, I feel.'

'What on earth do you mean?' She pushed past him into the room, for she could hear that Mary's anguish now seemed to be bordering on sobs. She was sitting on the bed, wringing her hands. Elena was trying to console her.

'Mary! What's the matter?' cried Kate.

'It's Paul. He's disappeared. I just left him, having his afternoon nap. I fell asleep too, out on the verandah, and when I woke up he'd gone.'

'But he can't be far,' insisted Kate.

A voice came from behind her. 'We have already searched the grounds. It seems that he has taken it into his head to go walkabout—while you were sunning yourself on the rocks.' The doctor paused and eyed her sardonically. 'I see you have burnt yourself. It happens to a lot of English tourists.'

'Never mind that,' snapped Kate, stung by his denunciation. 'Have you looked in the other rooms? He occasionally sits in the cool of the dining-room to write letters during the afternoon.'

'Naturally,' he replied laconically, but she had rushed from the room and along the verandah. She realised that of course they would have checked the other rooms in the villa, but she needed to collect her thoughts—away from the intimidating stare of the doctor.

Paul Jollison could not possibly have gone far, she reasoned, looking into bathroom, kitchen and dining room. The spaces left by the dining chairs she was still using for exercise therapy stared vacantly back at her. She stood in the doorway, something nagging away at the back of her mind. She slowly made her way back along the verandah, frowning.

The chairs, she thought. The exercises. Something Paul Jollison had said. A memory triggered and she turned and ran down the terraces of the garden.

'I have already investigated in that direction.' She ignored his dismissive shout. 'It is the track to the road which we should search,' he added, but she had vanished through the gate.

She slowed and stepped along the path, peering to left and right, trying to discern some movement amongst the lattice work of shadows cast by the tree branches.

There was nothing. She reached the cliff tops and stared worriedly about her. He could not have come this far. He would have tired far back. She returned and retraced her steps, this time stepping in amongst the trees from one side of the path to the other.

There! She craned her neck for a clearer view. She could make out a leg, encased in her patient's favourite brown trousers, and a foot in a suede boot. She darted forward, her pulse quickening.

He was sitting with his back resting against the

bole of a tree, his legs stretched out before him, the walking stick propped against the trunk. His face wore a serene expression and he was sleeping peacefully, his chest rising and falling in a gentle rhythm. Suddenly his eyes opened and he was looking up at her, his expression bright and alert.

'The blossom. Isn't it wonderful?' He raised his arms and gestured about him in wonderment.

'Yes, Mr Jollison, it is, but you have given us all the most fearful fright,' she said sternly.

'I have?' He stared at her incredulously.

'You've been gone for almost two hours, you know. Mary's very upset.'

'Oh dear. I had no idea.' He reached for his stick and began struggling to get up.

'Here.' She bent down and put a supporting arm under his. 'You should have left a note or waited until I came with you.'

'I suppose I should,' he said. 'But I couldn't resist it, Kate. Mary was dozing happily on the verandah. I didn't want to disturb her and it seemed only a short stroll down here. I was just sitting against the tree, being very grateful to be alive and surrounded by such beauty. Must have fallen asleep,' he ended ruefully, looking at her for forgiveness like some contrite child.

'Quite so,' said Kate with studied seriousness, but then softened and added, 'I'm in trouble with the doctor myself, you know, for doing the same thing on the beach.'

'The doctor's visiting is he? Oh dear. I seem to have caused a lot of trouble.'

'I think we should make our way back now,' went on Kate. 'You'll be surprised at how far it seems on the return trip. There's absolutely no hurry, but

Mary will be glad to have you back safe and sound.' She glanced sidelong at him. 'I take it you feel OK?'

He grinned at her. 'Giddiness or dizzy spells, you mean?' She nodded. 'None at all, m'dear, none at all. Well on the way to recovery now, don't you think?'

She smiled agreement and, taking his arm, led him through the trees to the track.

Mary was indeed glad to have her husband back safe and sound. After explanations had been briefly made, everything began to return to normal. Dr de Kerouac was still absent, however, presumably searching the landward side of the grounds, up towards the road.

'I'll try and find him,' said Kate, 'and I think we could all do with a cup of tea. I'll go across and tell Elena everything's all right now. Perhaps she'll put the kettle on.'

She was saved the task of looking for him, however, for he reappeared at the courtyard gates as she was going across to the kitchen.

'It's all right. I've found Mr Jollison,' she called.

He came up to her, an expression of concern on his face.

'Where is he? Is he hurt?'

'No, no. Not at all.' His concern was so disarming, that she was compelled to touch his sleeve in reassurance, but he stiffened and she hurriedly withdrew her hand, annoyed at herself for her involuntary gesture.

His concern had given way to a display of irritation. 'But where is he?' he repeated angrily.

Slightly hurt at her welcome news being received in this manner, she retreated into a more distant tone of voice. Apparently, his unjustified annoyance at her being responsible for Paul Jollison's *dis*appearance was now to be capped by even further annoyance at her being responsible for his *re*appearance. Well, two could play at that game.

'He's in his room,' she flared and turning, stalked off towards the kitchen.

'But where has he been?' he called after her.

Still smarting from his unwarranted behaviour, she continued on her way, flinging a 'Mary will explain' back over her shoulder.

She had no difficulty in communicating things to Elena, who gave her a hug, prefaced by some muttered prayer of thankfulness with her hands clasped together and eyes directed heavenwards. Kate indicated the teapot and kettle and receiving a nod of assent, returned to her room. She was still fuming inwardly and in no way inclined to join the conversation drifting in from the next room. On top of everything else, she could actually hear him laughing now. He sounded very relaxed.

She sat on the top step of the stairs leading up to the bed, feeling very humiliated. It was all so unfair. After all, she had only been gone for an hour or two. It could hardly be called dereliction of duty. It would be very necessary to maintain her defences with this temperamental man, she resolved. It would have been far more appropriate to have been congratulated on her progress with the patient. It was largely her encouragement and moral support that had given him the confidence to make his way down to the lemon grove in the first place.

She glumly folded her arms and then winced slightly. Her skin was really quite tender where she had caught the sun. She compressed her lips in annoyance as she remembered his reference to 'English tourists'. She stood up abruptly. This certainly would not do. She`was sitting in here practically in a sulk. Her eye caught her uniform, hanging neatly on the open wardrobe door. That was the answer, she thought. Wearing it, she could rejoin the group next door and face him with formal composure. It would also cover her distinctly pink upper arms, she smiled ruefully. She pulled the curtains and quickly changed.

'Ah, there you are, m'dear.' Paul Jollison greeted her warmly. 'Mary, pour our Kate a cup of tea.'

Kate smiled her thanks as Mary handed her a cup.

'I was just telling young de Kerouac here how well I'm feeling these days.'

Kate concealed her amusement at the pretentious doctor being referred to in such a casual manner. She sipped her tea primly. She had really turned the tables by donning her uniform. It was the doctor who seemed uncomfortable now, still dressed in his wind surfing gear. She raised her eyes from studying her cup to meet the gaze she could feel upon her.

Her rather unworthy smugness evaporated instantly at the open friendliness which shone out of his eyes.

'You are obviously a nurse of exceptional qualities, Katherine,' he said, perfectly seriously. 'Not many of my patients would set themselves such ambitious trips unaided. I think our problem with Mr Jollison will be more a need for restraint than for encouragement, *n'est-ce pas?*'

Mollified by this, she smiled warmly at him. Their eyes met and for a moment she was aware of nothing else but the frankness of the exchange. He seemed to be looking right into her. She had the distinct impression that he was remembering their confrontation down on the rocks and she felt the colour rising in her cheeks again. She hurriedly put down her cup and saucer on the tray and was furious when, of their own volition, they rattled noisily. She straightened and turned to Paul Jollison.

Displaying considerably more self-possession than she felt, she frowned at her patient. 'I think it's back to bed for a rest after all the excitement,' she pronounced.

'*Certainement*,' said the doctor, 'and I must be going. Perhaps Mrs Jollison would assist you, sir. Miss Trelawney can accompany me part of the way back to the cove. I would be intrigued to see just how far he did get on his little excursion.'

Before Kate could hesitate, she found herself ushered out on to the verandah. They negotiated the terraces of the garden and walked along the path into the trees. She led the way, very aware of his presence behind her.

She stopped. 'I think it was about here,' she said, pointing in amongst the foliage.

'Ah, yes. Some distance indeed after such a short time without crutches. You are to be congratulated on his progress, Katherine.'

There was a companionable silence.

'Actually, it was almost a shame to wake him,' she giggled. 'But I thought I'd better, what with everyone being so cross.'

'I think perhaps "concerned" would be a better

description.' The admonishment was gentle, but nevertheless noticeable.

'Yes.' She coloured slightly. 'I didn't mean . . . Well anyway, he was fast asleep, holding a lemon leaf between his fingers.'

'Had he crushed it?' He reached up and picked one. 'Here. The scent is at its very best if you crush it right under your nose.' He handed it to her.

She took it and did as he suggested. It was as though she breathed in the very essence of their surroundings. He took her hand and held it and the crushed leaf to his nostrils.

'I never tire of the fragrance,' he smiled at her. She experienced again that extraordinary jolt as their eyes met, as if an electric current had passed between them. For an absurd moment, she thought he was going to brush his cheek over the back of her hand. She held her breath.

Abruptly, his mood changed. '*Enfin*. It is time I returned.'

'Oh—yes,' she stammered. 'You are sailing your wind surfer back to Kalami?' She was still puzzled as to where he had appeared from when she had been sunbathing.

'No, not all the way to Kalami. I have my yacht moored just around the headland. It is a good anchorage.'

'Oh, I see.' She paused. 'Then you will have a following wind on your return journey. The onshore breeze is quite strong now. It will be a good sail.'

He was staring at her. 'You wind-surf?' he asked, eyebrows raised in surprise.

'Well no, not wind-surf exactly,' she replied.

'But I know a little about boats and . . .' she trailed off.

'Perhaps, one day, I will give you a lesson.' He looked her up and down. 'But not now. You are incorrectly attired.'

His mock seriousness caught her unawares and then, seeing the humour dancing in his eyes, she burst out laughing. He joined in, the ludicrous combination of her uniform, his sailing clothes and their surroundings touching both their senses of humour.

They caught their breath.

'And your boat? Is it the *Nautor Swan* you were buying at the Boat Show in January?'

'Yes, it is.'

'What do you call her?'

'*Liberté*.'

'That means freedom, doesn't it?'

'*Oui*.' It was said with a shrug, dismissing any deep meaning in the name.

'And you keep her always at Kalami?'

'Not always. Sometimes in Corfu Town marina, sometimes in Petrossos. It depends. But Kalami is a good mooring and tomorrow I may go for a short cruise. It depends on crew.'

She nodded.

'You can almost see the moorings from the cliff top. Or the headland at least. Come. I will show you.' He turned and led the way out of the lemon grove to where she had earlier noted the fork in the path.

'There, you see. You can reach Kalami itself along that path.' He pointed Northwards along the headland. 'But myself, I go by sea. *A bientôt*.' And he was gone, leaping from rock to rock down the winding cliff steps. It was as if a rather powerful force had left her.

She sat on a nearby sunwarmed rock, still feeling faintly ridiculous in her uniform. She unclipped the belt and slipped off the apron. At least it was just a ward dress now and she was not wearing cap or tights. He had reached the wind surfer and was stooping to remove a screw lid from a plastic cylinder lashed to the deck. It was obviously some sort of waterproof container, for he slipped off his leather sandals and towelling parka and stowed them. As he straightened she caught a glimpse of a wiry mat of black hair on his chest and a flat, tautly muscled stomach—then he was slithering the sailboard down the beach and towing it into deep water. She had come to realise from his air of maturity and confidence that he must be at least ten years older than her, but for a man well into his thirties he was remarkably lean and agile.

He paused and looked up at her. She acknowledged his wave of farewell. Then, in one movement, he was aboard and leaning back to pull the sail up and out of the water in one fluid movement. He paused to adjust the angle of the mast and his position on the board and then leaned back to take the full strength of the wind. He made it appear effortless. Within seconds he had got the board planing away out to sea, correcting the variations of the wind with gentle shifts of his weight and position. She felt a pang of envy at his skill—and the exhilaration of it. He was obviously very at home with the water. She watched as the surfer grew smaller in the distance until all she could make out was the brightly striped sail. Then that too disappeared round the headland.

*   *   *

The next day promised to be even hotter and Kate was awake early. She had not slept very well and had fleeting recollections of jumbled dreams. The doctor had figured prominently, but the images were confused and his presence all mixed up with her life in London. She had visited him on his yacht, but it was on dry land and when she stepped down into the cabin it had somehow turned into a hospital room, with Paul Jollison lying ill on the bunk. She felt jaded and tired.

After breakfast, her patient seemed rather listless.

'It's all the exertion and excitement of yesterday,' she admonished him gently. 'I think a quiet day in bed is prescribed. We'll give the exercises a miss.'

As a result of this, she found her morning was rather empty and she wandered round the villa with an odd sense of restlessness. Naturally a very active girl, she found periods of idleness were not to her liking. This would have been a perfect day for a wind surfing lesson, she mused. But the doctor's offer to teach her had seemed half-hearted, to say the least. But it had been voiced with an air of friendliness and the idea of messing about in boats with him as a companion was unexpectedly attractive.

She idly turned over the pile of books she had bought on a London bookshop excursion before leaving and selected a historical novel. It was much too nice to sit indoors to read and she went to sit out on the terrace. That would mean sharing Mary's company, however, and somehow she was not in the mood for joining in the normal trivial chatter. She paused by her verandah door hesitantly. She could not sit right out in the sun either. Her slightly burned skin needed a respite if she was to avoid unsightly peeling.

Then an idea struck her. It was the perfect time of day for a walk, before the full heat of the midday sun. If she put on one of her long sleeved cotton dresses, her skin would be protected.

She swiftly slipped into the dress and poked her head out of her door to tell Mary what she planned.

'I'll only be an hour or so,' she said. 'I thought I'd walk along the high path to Kalami headland. It looks as though the view might be worth the walk.' A small, mischievous voice within wanted to add that her inquisitiveness as to the whereabouts of a yacht named *Liberté* was also a motivating factor, but she thrust this ridiculous notion aside. She picked up her novel. She could always change her mind and settle for a quiet read in some suitably shady spot.

She put on her sunglasses and went down through the garden. Mary was immersed in some complicated piece of embroidery and absent-mindedly acknowledged her departure. Paul was sleeping and Mary was practically mounting guard over him to prevent any more walkabouts.

She reached the fork in the path and set off along the cliff top. The way rose and fell, clinging to the hillside and winding in and out of tumbled heaps of rock. She was very aware of the solitude, for apart from a sail or two on the horizon, she was alone with the shimmering heat and noise of the cicadas in the dry grass bordering the way.

Looking ahead, she caught the glint of the sun reflecting off something shiny. It could only be the top of a yacht's mast, although the boat itself was hidden from view by the headland. He had left it late if he intended to go for a Sunday sail, she mused, but perhaps his crew had not turned up. There was hardly any wind however and this was probably the reason for his still being at anchor. If indeed it was his yacht whose mast she could see.

The path led up a steep incline and when she reached the top she was able to see the boat quite clearly about two hundred yards away. She stopped and looked down with interest into the little bay.

It was undoubtedly a *Nautor Swan*. The sleek, expensive lines and distinctive bow confirmed that. It *was* also his boat, for the name *Liberté* was clearly visible on the large canvas spray shields carried by ocean-going yachts.

These points of identification seemed unimportant however, compared with the focal point of her attention—a pair of long legs stretched out along the deck, obviously very brown and obviously very female. A red bikini bottom clung to curved hips. Kate compressed her lips. At least it was apparently not lack of a crew which was preventing his Sunday cruise.

She could not make out any more of the sunbather, for her head and top half were obscured by the doctor himself. He had his back to Kate and was crouched on his haunches, in the act of placing a tall glass from which a straw projected, on to the cabin top. He was wearing swimming trunks and deck shoes. The sound of a laugh, rather gushing, floated up on the still air. He stood up and began picking his way back along the side deck towards the cabin entrance. Kate's gaze was transfixed, her eyes unable to tear themselves away from the cabin top and the female figure which was now leaning up on one elbow, languidly reaching for the drink.

It was not so much the shock of recognising the rather pouting features as belonging to Madeleine. Much more arresting was the sight of her full breasts without even the tiniest scrap of a bikini top covering them. Even more taunting was their deep rich tan—obviously the result of much exposure such as this to the warm Corfu sun.

Kate turned and fled back along the path, shocked and angry but thankful that neither of them had seen her. Clearly, Madeleine was more than just a casual acquaintance of the doctor's. Good heavens, he must be practically old enough to be her father, despite his youthful good looks. He would certainly be a connoisseur of topless sunbathers by now, thought Kate, furiously remembering her embarrassment of the previous afternoon. She could find no real reason for her sense of outrage, but strode along the way back to the villa, wanting to put as much distance as possible between her and the intimate tête a tête which she had unintentionally witnessed.

CHAPTER SIX

ON THE doctor's housecall the next day, Kate found
little difficulty in maintaining a formal approach.
Had she been less preoccupied with her own aloof-
ness she might have noticed the slight puzzlement
on his face at her manner, which bordered on the
icy.

She had mentioned to him that Paul Jollison had
woken up with a slight headache that morning.

'It is probably still the after effects of the concus-
sion, especially after his exertions of the other day.'
His eyes searched hers. 'And yourself, Katherine
. . . You are feeling well? You seem preoccupied.'

Despite her strongest efforts, she was not able to
meet his stare directly and fixed her gaze on a point
just above his head.

'I am perfectly well, thank you,' she said levelly.
His use of her name unshortened was somewhat
distracting. His accent made the 'th' sound more
like a 't'. She gave herself a mental shake.

'When will you visit next?' Her tone was now
almost peremptory.

'Well, it will be several days this time. I have to
visit Paxos later this week. It's a neighbouring
island,' he added. He stood there, inviting her to
ask more, but she remained silent. '*Enfin*, you will
be OK?'

'Naturally.'

'Well, until next week, then. Spiro will know
how to reach me in any emergency.'

'I doubt if there will be any need for that. Good afternoon.' She turned and went back into her room. To her utter astonishment, she felt herself shaking as she shut the door behind her. How ridiculous to let him make her angry, she told herself.

She heard his car start up and reverse out of the coutyard. She really must not let him affect her like this. After all, he was merely a rather superficial pleasure seeker, obviously quite prosperous, who liked to spend his money on fast cars, expensive yachts and easy-moralled young women. And Madeleine really *was* young, she reflected. Not more than eighteen or so, despite her well-endowed proportions. Crew indeed. Crewing aboard the *Liberté* probably involved all sorts of extra duties.

Good heavens, she was almost sniffing in disdain, like some narrow-minded spinsterly matron. This really would not do. If the arrogant French doctor liked to indulge himself idling around the Mediterranean with nubile young women for company, that was his affair. Her contact with him need only be purely professional.

She thrust him from her thoughts and then spent the hour or so before supper writing a long letter to her parents. Normally a good letter writer, she found inspiration difficult and, on reading it back, decided that she had certainly not made her impressions of Corfu sound very interesting. She decided to leave it unfinished and return to it the next day, hopefully with renewed enthusiasm.

Dinner was not exactly a satisfactory meal, for Paul Jollison had little appetite and after picking at his food, requested her help in getting back to bed.

He was still troubled by his headache and Kate gave him some Paracetamol.

He seemed brighter in the morning but on the day after, the headache was back with a vengeance. He was now describing it as a pain between the eyes only partly alleviated by the analgesics, which she had stepped up to codeine.

'Do you think you should send for the doctor, dear?' Mary's question, voicing Kate's own thoughts precisely, was unexpectedly irritating. She slipped a thermometer between his lips and, raising a finger to her mouth for silence, took his pulse. She entered the readings on his charts. Everything seemed normal. Why then was she agonising? She did not usually find it difficult to make decisions involving the doctor. And Mary's anxieties were not helping her husband at all, she knew.

'We will leave him to rest, Mary. Come and sit on the verandah.' She took her by the arm and firmly led her from the room. 'I'm just popping over to the kitchen to have a word with Elena.'

It would do no harm to investigate what was entailed in contacting Dr de Kerouac. At least she might have a telephone consultation with him.

Elena was preparing breakfast whilst Spiro sat at the table reading a newspaper.

She knocked on the open door. Spiro, anticipating an opportunity to practise his English, stood up and indicated another chair for her.

'Good morning, Nurse Trelawney,' he said.

She declined his offer of a chair. 'Is there a telephone number for the doctor?' she asked.

'Telephone doctor? There is a problem?' His face furrowed with concern and he turned to Elena.

'No—there is no problem—' Kate hastened to correct this impression but it was too late. Spiro and Elena engaged in one of their incomprehensible exchanges. Elena was drying her hands on her apron, coming towards Kate and asking unintelligible questions.

Suddenly, in the midst of all this confusion, another voice intruded.

'Nurse, Nurse, come quickly.' It was Mary, practically hysterical, calling from across the courtyard.

The trio in the kitchen stood stockstill, then as one person, rushed out.

Mary was standing outside her room, wringing her hands. 'Oh Kate, it's Paul. He just seemed to fall over.' Kate tore past her.

Paul Jollison was half-sitting, half-lying in the doorway to the bathroom. He held a hand to his head and was moaning incomprehensibly. Kate crouched down by his side and took his hand. He looked at her blankly at first, but then his eyes cleared.

'What happened?' he mumbled.

'It looks as though you felt a bit wobbly,' said Kate lightly, trying to conceal her concern.

'The room went all black and then . . .' He winced. 'It's this headache, Kate. It's a blinder.'

'Yes, I know. Don't worry. Let's get you back into bed, tucked up and comfortable. Then we'll sort you out.' She motioned to Spiro, who was hovering in the doorway, to help her lift Mr Jollison to his feet and over to his bed.

'I telephone Doctor now?' he enquired.

'Yes, I think so. I'll come across and talk to him myself.'

Spiro left the room nodding and gesticulating to

Elena. Kate turned back to her patient and settled him back.

'Now just try and relax. I think we'll have another codeine and then Mary will sit quietly with you while I go and talk to Dr de Kerouac.'

The telephone was in the kitchen and as she sped back across the courtyard, she could hear Spiro's voice bellowing down the receiver. She joined Elena and they both waited impatiently for him to finish.

He turned towards them, a look of concern on his face.

'Paxos,' he said. 'Dr de Kerouac on Paxos.' He turned and spoke into the receiver again.

Dismayed, Kate recalled his last visit, when he had spoken of his intended trip.

'But is it far? When can he come?' She was standing at Spiro's elbow now trying to make herself understood. What she would give for some help in interpreting now, even from Madeleine. Spiro was holding a hand up to still her questions, straining to hear what both she and his telephone party were saying and trying to speak himself—all at the same time. Everything was utterly impossible. At last, he put the receiver down.

'Dr de Kerouac, he come,' he announced.

'But when?'

'I speak his office. They ring him in Paxos. They have telephone number. You understand?'

'Yes, yes.' Kate fought to control her impatience for fear of breaking his painful concentration.

'But telephone lines not good in the mornings.' He shook his head but then rushed on headlong as he saw the dangerous glint in her eye. 'They ring. They ring. He catch ferry, perhaps midday—'

'Perhaps?'

'—then I go meet him in Corfu town. He not have his car with him.'

'But what time will he get here?'

Spiro was doing laborious counting exercises on his fingers.

'Four o'clock,' he announced finally.

It was pointless to remonstrate. The effort of communication was too exhausting and she would need all her energy to keep Paul Jollison calm—*and* his wife, she thought wearily.

By the middle of the afternoon he had developed a slight temperature, but Kate had managed to make him comfortable by keeping the room shaded and applying frequent cold compresses to his forehead. Elena maintained a constant supply of iced water from the kitchen. It was with relief that she heard two doors slam outside on the Peugeot, signalling Spiro's arrival with the doctor.

The door opened and he entered. She felt again that sensation of being in the presence of a powerful force. He was wearing a pair of casual navy slacks and a short sleeved cotton shirt. A light coloured linen jacket was slung round his shoulders. If anything, his tan seemed deeper. He appraised the darkened room and the cold compress on Paul Jollison's forehead in an instant.

'A small problem, yes?' he said.

'Well, I wasn't sure whether to call you or not—especially all the way from Paxos, but—'

'Please, Nurse Trelawney. You misunderstand me,' he interrupted. He moved to the bed, placing his medical bag on a chair. Kate gently ushered Mary from the room and then stood at the bottom of the bed.

'Now then, Mr Jollison. I am told you had a little dizzy spell.' He had taken Jollison's wrist and was checking his pulse.

'It was silly of me, Doctor. Sorry to cause such a fuss. It's this headache really. I can hardly think straight.'

'Do not worry. We'll soon take care of things.' He indicated for Kate to pass him the monitoring charts. 'One thing is for certain. It cannot be nearly as serious as Spiro made out to me on the car journey up from Corfu Town.' His light humour broke the tension in the room. Even Paul smiled ruefully.

Kate felt a sense of relief. She realised she had been worrying quite unnecessarily about summoning him. He obviously felt she had done the right thing. She watched as he conducted a full examination.

Eventually he stood back, thinking deeply, tugging gently at his ear lobe with finger and thumb. Finally he made a decision.

'I would like, with Nurse's help, to make one last little test, Mr Jollison. You may not find it comfortable, but there will be no cause for concern.'

'Anything you say, Doctor.'

'*Bon.* Now Nurse, some help please.'

Together they manoeuvred Mr Jollison so that he was sitting on the edge of the bed, legs dangling.

'Nurse, perhaps you would be so kind as to just kneel on the bed behind Monsieur. No, do not support him unless he needs it.' Kate did as she was asked as he turned to their patient.

'Now, I want you to follow this pencil with your eyes. Do not move your head, just your eyes. I will hold it straight in front of you at first, then move it from side to side.'

'It hurts when I strain my eyes across,' complained Jollison as the pencil moved to one side.

'Mm, yes. And now follow the pencil to the other side, if you will.'

Jollison did as he was asked—and suddenly fell backwards. Kate was taken completely unawares and only just managed to support him.

'Do not worry, Monsieur. It is as I suspected. A little virus, that is all. Nurse will make you comfortable again and then I will explain.' He turned and searched in his bag. He came back with a small bottle of pills.

'You have picked up a little bug which is affecting your inner ear. It is only temporary.'

'But I can hear you perfectly well, Doctor—'

'Yes I know. But your ear also affects your sense of balance. The virus has upset the little mechanism in one ear, The otolith organ, *n'est-ce pas*, Katherine?'

Pleased to be a party to his diagnosis, she nodded and smiled at Jollison. 'I expect Doctor will give us some antibiotics for it.'

He passed her the bottle of pills.

'As long as it cures the headache, Doctor,' said Jollison.

'I am certain that will disappear with the virus.'

He packed his bag and together they made their way across the quadrangle.

'That is a relief,' she said simply. 'I was a little concerned. I've seen a rather nasty case of recurring epilepsy after a skull fracture.'

'Ah yes, *le petit mal*. No, it is nothing like that I am sure. You did quite right to call me though, Katherine.'

The pleasant shared feeling of being colleagues, together with his use of her Christian name in that odd accent of his was very disturbing. She looked up to see his smiling gaze upon her and her heart turned over.

'Er, would you like a cup of tea before you—I mean I could ask Elena.' To her amazement she was practically stammering.

'Ah, the English cup of tea.' He was grinning like some cheeky schoolboy. '*Mais non, merci*. I must have Spiro drive me to my car.'

'I am sorry to have spoilt your trip to Paxos. I am told it is a beautiful island.'

'It is beautiful,' he agreed. 'But I had finished my work, so it was no inconvenience.'

'Your work? But I assumed . . .'

'That it was a pleasure trip?' He had stiffened slightly.

'No, I didn't mean . . .' She was furious at herself for having clumsily broken the friendly atmosphere of professional collaboration.

'There is an orphanage there run by the nuns. It is a charity organisation, unlike your English welfare state.' A note of scorn had entered his voice. She remained silent, not wanting to provoke him further.

'I hold a clinic there every two weeks or so. It is my way of helping the nuns in their work.'

There was an awkward silence.

Trying to recapture their earlier mood, Kate responded, 'That must be really useful work. I sometimes feel that I . . .' She trailed off.

'Would like to do something more worthwhile?' he finished for her.

'Well yes,' she rejoined, almost defensively. 'As

a matter of fact, I should very much like to visit your orphanage clinic. If you should ever need any help, that is.' What on earth was she saying? She stared at the ground.

'Perhaps one day, when Mr Jollison is fully recovered. But there is nothing much to see. Ah, here is Spiro.' He had turned and was getting into the Peugeot.

'Ring me in a day or so and tell me how your patient is. I will not come unless you think it necessary.'

She was left feeling a slight sense of anti-climax.

By the next week, Paul Jollison was fully recovered and there had been no need to call the doctor. Not only had every trace of the virus disappeared, but he seemed to have developed a new lease of strength as a result of his enforced return to bed. He was now quite confident to be moving all around the villa with his walking stick.

A milestone in his progress one day was a walk, accompanied by Mary, to the cliff at the top of the cove where Kate now regularly went sunbathing.

'The next stage is to get you down there swimming,' she promised. 'Best therapy of all.' She saw a mischievous gleam in his eye. 'But no attempting anything like that until I say so,' she warned sternly.

'Yes, Nurse,' said Paul Jollison obediently. She could see he meant it.

They returned to the villa to find that the doctor had telephoned.

'He ask about Mr Jollison,' explained Spiro. 'I

tell him OK but he still want you to telephone him. Tonight, after he finished seeing patients.'

As they sat round the table after dinner, Kate felt a thrill of anticipation at the prospect of speaking to him. She went across to the kitchen and could hardly contain her impatience while Spiro went through the complicated business of obtaining the number.

At last he handed her the receiver. 'The doctor,' he announced proudly.

'Ah Katherine.' His voice sounded oddly metallic on the ancient instrument. '*Comment ça va?*'

'Everything's fine, thank you, Dr de Kerouac,' she replied.

'Your patient. He is better I presume? You have not felt it necessary to call me.'

'No, we're doing very well. Walks to the cliff top are now routine.'

'*Bon.*' He paused and she waited expectantly. He could not have asked her to call merely to discuss Paul Jollison's progress.

'I have to go to Paxos on Saturday, to the orphanage I mentioned.'

'I see.' There was another silence.

'If you were interested,' he went on, 'I wondered if you would care to come?' He was hesitant. 'You did say you would like to pay it a visit. You might find it enjoyable to meet some of the children—and the nuns. They are good friends of mine. If you are confident about leaving Mr Jollison, of course.'

She interrupted him 'I should love to come,' she replied.

'*Bon.*' Was it her imagination or had his voice lifted slightly? 'We will catch the ferry at ten o'clock. You can ask Spiro to drive you. Can you be at the terminal in Corfu Town by nine-thirty?'

'Of course.'

'Well, until Saturday then. Oh, I almost forgot. I am planning to come back on *Liberté*. You do not object to that mode of transport?'

'No, no, of course not. As a matter of fact, I just love—'

'Excellent. Let's hope you do not suffer from sea-sickness. *Au revoir.*'

Her reply died in her throat as she heard the metallic buzz which signified the end of the call. She replaced the receiver, feeling a little stunned, but with a sense of mounting excitement. She and Mary had dug out one of the guide books in the villa and read all about Paxos. It was much smaller than Corfu, with only a fraction of the population. A holiday isle really, but at this time of the year it would be virtually empty. It sounded delightful. And a chance to do a little sailing. She had not realised he had taken the trip out in *Liberté*. That meant he would have been without his yacht for almost two weeks as a result of her emergency call for him to return by ferry. But he had not mentioned it at all. It must have been very inconvenient to leave the yacht behind.

She wondered if he had sailed out single-handed. Or, gloomy thought, perhaps Madeleine had crewed for him . . .

She shook herself free from this rather tedious conjecture and tripped across to her room to examine her wardrobe and see if she could find a suitable combination of clothes to take and wear. Who cared if Madeleine had helped him to sail *Liberté* out to Paxos? It was she, Kate, who had been asked to sail on the return trip and she had been delighted to accept. After all, she was only going for the pleasure of a little sight-seeing and sailing, she told herself firmly.

CHAPTER SEVEN

SATURDAY morning found Kate in Corfu Town even earlier than the prescribed nine-thirty. She had found a very adequate wardrobe for both the ferry trip out and the sail back. The clothes for the latter were neatly packed in her flight bag—a pair of jeans, a spare sweater and her zip-up anorak in case it got chilly. The only thing she lacked was a pair of deck shoes. She was not going to invite his ridicule by turning up and expecting to tread on the beautiful teak decks of the *Swan* with ordinary town shoes. Nor were the light blue casual shoes she was wearing really suitable.

The Jollisons had explained to her that the Greek shops opened particularly early in the morning to make up for the traditional afternoon siesta. She had guessed correctly that there would be a yacht chandlers near the port at Corfu and was easily able to purchase a pair of proper sailing docksiders with some of her Greek currency.

If the weather were hot enough, she would be able to go barefoot anyway, possibly be able to swim as well. But she had decided not to bring her bikini for she had freely admitted to herself that she had no intention of reminding him of other, more free and easy, shipmates.

Still, it was a pity not to be able to go swimming if the opportunity arose, she mused and then, on an impulse, tried on and bought a very simple but classically cut one-piece costume. It was in a royal

blue, a colour which suited her well and it fitted
excellently on her slim hips with a nicely styled
shape to the top of the leg. It was also flattering to
the soft lines of her bosom. It was not often she
thought about buying something, tried it on and
knew instantly and confidently that it looked good
and suited her, she thought. She skipped out of the
shop, the lightness in her heart echoed by the spring
in her step, and went in search of the boarding gate
where she would presumably find him waiting for
her.

She spotted him immediately, buying tickets at
the cash window. She stood at his elbow and waited
for him to pick up his change and turn to see her.

'Ah, Katherine,' he smiled. *'Bonjour.'*

'Et bonjour aussi,' she ventured. It was a
pleasant relaxed meeting. He steered her towards
the ferry gangplank, hoisting a bright yellow sailing
holdall up on to one shoulder.

'You are looking very cool this morning, Nurse
Trelawney,' he said, stepping back as they walked,
to appraise her denim skirt and blue and white
striped t-shirt. She felt crisp and neat and knew that
the tan she had developed looked well on her legs
and arms. Nevertheless, she coloured slightly and
greeted his compliment with a demure thank you.

He stood aside to allow her to step up on to the
gangplank.

'How long does the crossing to Paxos take?' she
asked.

'About two hours. It is a pleasant trip and the sea
is calm today.' She could hear him treading up the
ramp behind her.

They reached the passenger deck and she looked
around with interest. It was quite a modern ferry

and it contrasted oddly with the ancient architecture of the old town and port. She peered over the side rail at the bustle of activity going on around the entrance to the ship's hold. A number of commercial vehicles were being driven aboard, together with last minute items of cargo, building materials and several packing cases.

'All the islands are very dependent upon boats to bring them the necessities of life.' He was standing at her side. 'People often forget what a seafaring race the Greeks need to be.'

'Fishermen, too,' she added, pointing towards the fleet of colourful caiques moored in the inner harbour.

'Yes indeed,' he replied. 'Now, where would you like to sit? It is pleasant up here on deck, you agree? Also, I can show you points of interest more easily.'

Very soon, the last few items of cargo had been brought aboard and the rumble of engines and churning water round the ferry's stern as the propeller began to turn signalled their departure. They passed out through the harbour entrance and began to feel the gentle effect of the light Mediterranean swell. The voyage passed quickly and, as promised, he drew her attention to a number of features as they made their way down the curving Corfu coastline. At one point, she thought he was making fun of her, for he pointed across at some low-lying ground to the South of the port and said, 'That's where the Corfu cricket ground is situated.'

She looked at him in disbelief.

'It's true,' he said. 'The Greeks have a cricket team here. Surely every English person knows that?' He was grinning at her and she shook her head.

'I promise you,' he laughed. 'It is a hangover from the days when Corfu was a British Protectorate, under Queen Victoria.'

'All right, I believe you,' she said and then they were both laughing.

They made their landfall on Paxos at a tiny fishing village called Lacca. It seemed as though they were approaching impenetrable rocks as they closed the island, but at the last minute the cliffs opened up and she caught a glimpse of tiny white houses through the narrow entrance. Then they were through and into a delightful little natural harbour, completely sheltered from the open sea.

'And there is *Liberté*.' In his excitement at seeing his yacht safely at anchor still, he had slid one arm under hers and was pointing with the other at the *Swan*, which was lying peacefully to a mooring buoy in the far corner of the cove. He seemed unaware of his animated behaviour, but the touch of his cool grasp on her arm was electrifying. She slipped her sunglasses back on to cover her confusion.

'She is beautiful, do you not think?' He was walking Kate round the deck, intent on keeping the yacht in view as the ferry swung round and began to manoeuvre up towards the tiny quay. There was an earsplitting blast on the ship's siren and ropes were run ashore and secured.

'It is the main event of the day—the arrival of the ferry,' he observed as they allowed the colourful disembarkation of people and vehicles to precede them. Then they too made their way ashore.

'We should go straight to the orphanage,' he said. 'There are several children I would like to see and we do not wish to leave our return journey too late. I make it a point to try not to sail after dark with an inexperienced crew.'

'You really don't need to worry about—' But she was addressing her remarks to his retreating back. She sighed in mild exasperation. She really would have to set the record straight with him about her sailing experience. He had stopped and was looking down puzzledly from a narrow flight of steps leading up through the little houses. '*Allons*. It is this way,' he said.

She caught up with him and together they climbed up through several levels until they stood before two large wooden gates set in a stone wall. They rang the bell and were greeted by a smiling Sister and led into a cool, tiled room.

She had wondered about his lack of a medical bag on the ferry journey but it soon transpired that the room had been converted into a well equipped surgery. He unlocked the pharmacy cabinet and she caught a glimpse of a comprehensive stock of medicine and drugs.

Much to Kate's astonishment, the Sister Theresa who had greeted them turned out to be very Irish, although she was apparently fluent in Greek.

'It's fairly healthy we all are this time, Doctor, so we've not much for you to attend to on your visit. Although the children will be pleased to see you, sure enough. To say nothing of your pretty companion.' She smiled at Kate. 'It's not every day the children meet someone with such fair hair,' she explained. She patted the back of a chair. 'Why don't you sit here, Nurse Trelawney, while I help the Doctor with his record cards.'

Kate sat patiently—and with some interest—as his young patients were individually brought in.

They were all absolutely charming and rather shy at seeing a strange face. The doctor however was obviously well-known to them and she noted the easy, relaxed way he had with the children, soon putting them at their ease.

Eventually the procession of patients ended and he turned to Sister Theresa.

'And now, how is little Maria?'

'Well, Doctor, she has been causing us some concern sure enough. We've been keeping her in bed, not that she's shown much inclination to be up and about. She's been complaining of pains in her neck and a sore throat and headache.'

'I think I should see her, don't you?'

They went along a corridor and into a room containing several beds. In one of them lay a pretty little dark-eyed girl. She displayed only a flicker of interest at seeing them.

'Yes, looking a little poorly, I think.' He reverted into some gentle questions in Greek and Maria nodded.

'I would like to examine her. Perhaps, Sister Theresa, we could sit her up.'

He pulled out his stethoscope and listened to respiration and cardiac beat. Then he gently probed around the child's throat. She was obviously uncomfortable and when he applied the gentlest of pressure to the side of her neck, she began to whimper.

Kate's sympathy overcame her and she stepped forward to comfort the little girl. To her surprise, two tiny arms were immediately entwined around her neck and a tear-streaked face buried in her shoulder. She muttered consoling sounds and gradually the sniffs diminished.

The doctor's face was concerned. 'Her neck's very tender. I rather think she has a gland infection. I am sorry, *ma petite*, I did not mean to hurt you.' He leaned forward and stroked the fine dark strands of hair. A pair of liquid brown eyes peered up at him and, seeing his smiling gaze, were shyly buried again with a twist of the head.

His lips were pursed. 'I will prescribe a short course of antibiotics, but I fear she could be displaying the early symptoms of glandular fever. We should really take a blood sample back to the laboratory in Corfu Town Hospital.' He frowned. 'But I do not think that Maria will easily allow me to take one.'

'Ah now, Doctor. It sounds like women's work. Do you not agree, Nurse Trelawney? You've taken dozens of samples I'll be bound.' Sister Theresa was looking at her, a confident expression on her face.

'Well yes, I have,' replied Kate, 'but . . .'

'Well it's easy then, isn't it Doctor? Will I be giving her a little cuddle, while you and Nurse Trelawney fetch what you need from the surgery?'

In the face of such common sense, Kate and the doctor withdrew.

Back in the surgery, he delved in the pharmacy cabinet and extracted a blood sample kit. 'You'll find a blood pressure armlet in the cupboard over there,' he said and sat down at the desk, pulling a pen from his pocket and making notes on a medical record card.

'But aren't you going to supervise?' she asked in surprise.

He looked up. 'Of course not,' he said lightly. 'I have not the slightest doubt that I can leave things to you. You have the touch, Katherine—and little Maria has taken to you.'

Delighted to be able to make herself useful, she sped back to the bedside and did as he had asked. Her ability to conceal the needle of the syringe was helped tremendously by Sister Theresa creating a diversion with the help of a large teddy bear.

'Well, she'll do, I think,' pronounced Kate at last, adroitly concealing the full syringe behind her.

'She will that, Nurse Trelawney,' said the nun as she pressed a swab to Maria's arm where Kate had made the venupuncture.

They retraced their way along the corridor back to the surgery.

'You are lucky to have such a fine surgery for the doctor to use when he visits,' commented Kate as they approached the door.

'Oh, but it is not ours, Nurse Trelawney. It is Dr de Kerouac's. We have merely provided the room. Everything in there has been donated by him to our charity.'

'Oh,' said Kate. 'I didn't realise. You mean he has provided all those drugs and medicines?'

'Every last one. He is a generous man, do you not think? We are very lucky.'

Any further discussion was curtailed as the door was opened to reveal the doctor waiting for them.

'*Ah bon,*' he said, seeing the blood sample in Kate's hand. 'All went well I see. You must come with me again, Nurse.'

'That she must, Doctor,' interjected Sister Theresa, unwittingly saving Kate the need for reply, for she suddenly found his light-hearted suggestion very appealing and she was not able to find a suitable reply.

'Perhaps you would just seal and tag the sample—and then we should prepare ourselves for the return trip,' he added.

'But you'll both have a little lunch with us? You must have time for something,' said Sister Theresa.

'That would be delightful, Sister,' he replied.

Half an hour later they were standing on the quay of the little fishing village, discussing a very different topic.

'Our only problem now is to locate *Liberté*'s dinghy,' he said wryly. 'The fishermen have probably had to move it to land their catches. *Ah voilà!*' He had spotted the little craft pulled up on the beach between two rowing boats.

Now and again a person becomes transformed as they adopt a role in which you have never seen them before. As though the rest of their life was spent simply marking time until they can do the one thing they love best. So it obviously was with the doctor and boats. As he pulled the dinghy carrying them both across to *Liberté* with long powerful strokes, it was as though he had become part of the craft, his long frame moulding to the seat, the oars into his hands, with the ease of long and frequent practice.

'She looks fine, *n'est-ce pas?*' He inclined his head in the direction of the yacht. 'A little more at home here than at the Boat Show.'

'She looks beautiful, Laurent,' replied Kate, for indeed she did. The clean lines of her hull were alive with the dappled reflections of the sun on the water. Kate peered over the side of the dinghy. 'I can even see the anchor chain stretching right down to the bottom. The water's so clear,' she exclaimed.

He was deftly manoeuvring the dinghy and turning it up and alongside the smooth white hull. 'I will hold us alongside while you climb aboard. Step from the middle of the dinghy, not the edge, or you will tip us in.'

She suppressed the rejoinder that she had clambered in and out of a hundred dinghies and, reaching up to the deck, nimbly pulled herself aboard.

He handed her up his holdall and her bag and then climbed up himself. Unbidden, she pulled the dinghy round to the back of the yacht and swiftly tied its rope to the stern rail. She turned to see a look of surprise on his face.

'I see you know how to tie proper knots,' he said. 'That will be useful.'

Now she would show him, she determined.

'I've done a bit of sailing with my father and brother,' she announced airily, 'so I do know a little.' She placed her hands on her hips, glanced up at the sky with the expression of a seasoned mariner and pressed home her advantage. 'Nice gentle Force Three breeze I would say. Looks as though we'll have it on our beam on the way back to Corfu. What sails are you going to set, skipper? Full mainsail and genoa?'

She looked back at him nonchalantly and found him staring at her, mouth agape. His astonishment was so genuinely disarming that she was unable to keep her face straight. Seeing her amusement, he too began to smile—and then they were both laughing openly.

'I see I have made a great error in assuming you were a novice, Katherine,' he said, when they had caught their breath. 'My apologies. It will be a delight to have a competent crew. Come, I will show you over the yacht.'

'I'd like to change into more suitable clothes first. I've some jeans and proper shoes.'

'Of course. In that case, we will start our tour down below in the cabin.' He paused. 'But, of course, you have seen the interior before, haven't you? Perhaps I should go first to make sure the companionway steps are securely fixed.' It was his turn to try and look serious and fail, for they burst out laughing again at the memory of their first meeting.

He disappeared below and she followed, rather aware of the unsuitable nature of the denim skirt for negotiating such awkward descents backwards. But when she reached the cabin floor, he court-eously had his back to her and was searching about on the chart table.

She looked around the cabin. It was difficult to believe it was the same one that she had investi-gated that day long ago in London. It was different now, full of his personal things. The bookshelves were crammed and the lockers full. It all looked very homely.

'You can use the cabin through here to change,' he said and stood aside to let her squeeze past.

The rear cabin was a smaller version of the main saloon. Presumably this was where he slept when he was on passage. She looked around at the beautifully moulded teak panelling. There were cushioned side seats and a wide berth, neatly made up with crisp white sheets and blue blankets. She examined the books stacked on the shelf at the head of the bunk. They were all to do with ships and the sea. A much-thumbed volume featured Eric

Tabarly, the French single-handed yachtsman—a hero of Kate's and obviously his as well.

'I'm going up on deck to start rigging the sails,' he called out.

'Coming,' she replied and shrugged herself out of her daydream. She had been wondering where members of the crew slept when he was not sailing alone—the well proportioned Madeleine, for example—but she dismissed these thoughts firmly. She was here for a pleasurable afternoon's sailing on the Ionian Sea. It would be a new experience—very unexpected, and one she was determined to enjoy.

She discovered him on the foredeck, pulling armfuls of canvas out of a sail bag. He was wearing his towelling parka and a pair of extremely faded denim shorts. He moved easily and assuredly as he worked. He straightened up and approvingly surveyed her attire as she approached. She felt much more comfortable in her jeans but rather wished her docksiders did not look quite so obviously new on her feet. They did not really match her claim to being a seasoned yachtswoman.

'I can be bending on the sails,' she offered. 'I am sure there are other things you could be doing.'

'Very well.' The approving look was there again. 'I will check the engine. We will motor out of the cove and hoist sail once we are outside.'

He moved back along the deck and she busied herself snapping on the stainless steel hooks and attaching the ropes which controlled the large headsail. She ran these back through the special pulleys to where they could be adjusted, next to the big gleaming steering wheel. Eventually, everything was ready.

'I will haul out the anchor,' he said and eyed her intently. 'You have experience of steering?' he enquired and she laughed, for he almost sounded apologetic, obviously trying to make up for his earlier misjudgment of her.

'Yes, I do. If you like, I can motor her up to the anchor as you haul it in. It will make it easier,' she offered. 'But you will just have to explain the engine controls. They are different from my father's boat.'

Between them, they left the anchorage as if with the skill of a team long accustomed to working together. She slowly edged the *Swan* up as he hauled in the chain with powerful swinging movements, his legs and arms braced against its weight. He stowed the anchor and came back to join her at the steering position in the cockpit. She made to move aside to let him take the wheel as the steady thump of the diesel engine propelled them out through the rocky harbour entrance, but he shook his head and indicated that she continue steering.

'Once we have passed the headland, we will hoist the sails. You agree?'

She nodded. His attitude to her had changed completely. He was treating her as an equal and she knew she was enjoying it.

He moved up to the bows again, carrying the heavy steel winch handle with which to haul the sails up tight. She expertly brought the yacht up into the wind as he pulled on the ropes. With a crackle of snapping canvas, the sails slid smoothly up the mast. She was able to anticipate his needs exactly and began to steer the boat off on to the right course as he rejoined her. The sails ceased their frantic flapping as the wind filled them. The

Swan began to heel gently and they were sailing. He came back and reached across to the engine's ignition switch.

'Now?' he enquired.

'Now!' she nodded, laughing, for she knew what came next.

'*Le moment tranquil*,' he said. The engine's roar died as he turned the switch.

'Exactly,' she breathed. She would never tire of this moment, successfully out of harbour, with the wind free, the sails pulling—and it was as if you were leaving all the clamour of the landbound world behind as you turned off the engine. He leaned across and adjusted some ropes and the *Swan's* bow began to rise and fall, cleaving its way through the blue water. Showers of spray pattered on the deck up ahead, the dancing droplets making little rainbows in the bright sunlight. To be sailing again—and here of all places. It was like nothing she had ever experienced before. She felt a great wave of exultation and lifted her face to the sun and ran a hand through her hair, sighing.

She realised he was looking at her and she smiled happily. He too wore a look of utter contentment.

'*La Liberté*,' she murmured.

He nodded and they shared a moment of complete understanding. She felt a shiver and rubbed the skin of her bare arms.

'You would like to steer?' she said suddenly.

'But no, not unless you wish me to.'

'Oh no. I just wondered . . .' She trailed off.

'It is a pleasure to have such an able companion, Katherine.'

'Well, I'm having a lovely time,' she smiled. 'It was very nice of you to ask me.'

'*Ça ne fait rien*,' he replied. 'Now then . . .' He reached into a locker and, pulling out a pair of binoculars, scanned the horizon. 'Our course is almost due North. If you steer about 20°, it will take us into the South Corfu channel.'

He had not even enquired if she knew how to sail a compass course, she realised. Flattered, she settled into a more comfortable position where she could see the compass in its burnished brass case and keep an eye on the sails at the same time.

And so the time passed. They chatted a little, mostly about boats, and she told him about her family and their ketch. She explained that she had crewed many times for her father.

'He would enjoy this,' she said. 'He has sailed in the Mediterranean, when he was stationed at Gibraltar, but never on a yacht like this. I know he has a high regard for the design.'

He asked her about sailing off the Cornish coast and listened with interest to her description of the famous Transatlantic races which started from Plymouth.

'I have seen many of your countrymen taking part,' she said. 'Even the great Eric Tabarly. The French produce many fine yachtsmen.'

'So does your country,' he insisted. 'Yachtswomen too. Your Clare Francis for example.'

They lapsed into a friendly silence, sharing the pleasure of the afternoon. In the distance, the coast basked in the sun.

As they made their way up past the southern tip of Corfu the wind began to drop. Her jeans were becoming very warm as the cooling effect of the breeze began to diminish. She began to feel uncom-

fortably sticky. She shifted her position and he
noticed her discomfiture.

'You will find some cold drinks in the refrigera-
tor,' he said. 'Here, I will take the helm while you
fetch them. There are also some rolls and cheese
and salad if you are hungry. I bought them in the
market at Corfu this morning. They're in one of the
side lockers next to the stove.' She moved aside
for him.

'You should have brought some shorts. It is often
hot here in the South Channel. The mainland shel-
ters us from the wind.'

She nodded ruefully and went towards the cabin
entrance. A thought struck her. 'I did bring a
swimming costume,' she added.

'Well, why not put it on? It will get even warmer
if the wind drops any more,' he said. 'But be careful
of the sun. I would use some cream, especially on
your shoulders.'

Was there a hint of mischief in his voice? A
teasing reminder of another occasion when they
had discussed the dangers of sunburn? She looked
back at him sharply, but he was peering up at the set
of the sails, his face innocent of any expression.

Down in the cabin, she made up her mind. The
swimming costume it would be. It could only add to
the pleasure of the beautiful afternoon. Swiftly, she
slipped out of her clothes and put it on, grateful to
get out of the jeans. She emerged from the cabin,
carrying the cans of soft drinks and rolls, to find that
he too was taking advantage of the sun and had
divested himself of his parka.

He stared at her, his eyes running over her trim
figure, and she felt her colour rising. She found his
frank appraisal disturbing and for a moment almost

regretted putting on the costume. The sails flapped suddenly as the *Swan* slid up into wind. He hastily resumed his concentration on the helm.

'I've brought the food and drink,' she said unnecessarily.

'Come and sit next to me. You can keep the hard-working helmsman supplied with sustenance.' He moved aside on the bench seat to make room for her. She was very aware of him as she took the offered place and passed him a frosted cold can. She could feel the pressure of his thigh against hers as they both braced their legs out to counteract the heel of the boat in the wind. The tan she had accumulated on her legs looked positively pale beside his.

He reached behind her to adjust a rope and she felt the mat of wiry hair on his chest brush against her shoulder. She averted her gaze, disturbed by their physical proximity, but he seemed unaware of it—a fact which she almost resented. Shocked at this thought, she sought a safe topic of conversation.

'It's getting hotter, if anything,' she ventured.

'Yes—and the wind is dropping fast. It will come back in the late afternoon—there is always a fresh breeze off the shore as the land begins to cool. But it will not come in time to get us into Corfu Town before dark. You do not mind?'

'No, not in the least. I enjoy sailing at night,' she replied.

He had lapsed into a contemplative silence.

'On the other hand,' he went on, 'there is a charming little fishing village called Petrossos on the western edge of Corfu. We could put in there for tonight and finish the trip tomorrow morning.

We would have time for a swim before evening perhaps.'

'That would be really lovely, but . . .'

'I could give you a lesson on the wind surfer. And there's a little taverna where we could have supper.'

'It sounds wonderful, Laurent, but what about the Jollisons? How would we let them know?'

'There is a telephone at the taverna. I will speak with Spiro. If there is the slightest doubt, he can drive across from Netriti and pick you up in the Peugeot. I can sail *Liberté* back on my own in the morning if necessary.'

'Well, if you're sure,' she said. She really hoped the Jollisons *would* be happy to be without her for one night, for the prospect of a swim and a leisurely Greek supper was very attractive. Apart from the party at the Stephens' villa, she had not eaten out at all since her arrival in Corfu.

'I think perhaps the wind is going to make up our minds for us,' he added and pointed up at the sails.

The breeze had dropped completely now and the sails were wrinkling, their former fullness gone. The *Swan* began to roll on the swell, the sails flapping noisily.

'We will need to put on the motor, just to make Petrossos,' he said. 'Will you take the helm, while I stow things?'

Thus the decision was made and any qualms she felt about spending the night alone aboard the yacht with him were banished by the activity of sail gathering and course changing. They had recaptured their mood of friendly companionship, the air of charged intimacy gone.

The motion of *Liberté* as she rolled on the

Mediterranean swell with no wind to give her life, had become quite marked and it was a relief when he flicked the engine into life and they began to punch through the sea again. The movement of their passage created a cooling wind and Kate stood by the mast enjoying its touch on her bare skin. She shaded her hand against the sun and looked out towards the distant shore.

At first the coast was just a hazy outline, but gradually she began to distinguish between the soaring peaks in the distance and the rocky out-crops and cliffs along the coastline as *Liberté* slowly closed the land. Soon she could see a jetty with moored fishing boats against a background of pine-wooded hills, through which were glimpses of white walled, square roofed buildings.

For some time now the sea had been a flat calm, like a mirror with only their passage to disturb its surface, but near the shoreline she could see a flurry of ripples moving out towards them.

'It is the land breeze I spoke of,' he shouted above the noise of the engine. She looked back at him and nodded.

'Where are we going to moor?' she mimed.

'At the jetty, between the fishing boats,' he yelled.

She made her way back to the cockpit to join him. He bent down to the throttle and reduced the engine's speed to a gentle putter.

'In the Mediterranean, one ties up with the bow to the wall and the stern sticking straight out. There is no up and down movement with tides and it makes more use of the space.' She had noticed that he had a habit of emphasising points with his hands whenever he was trying to explain something.

'Here, I will show you.' He rummaged around in a side locker and emerged with a small anchor and line.

'First of all, we aim the boat at the spot we have selected and throttle back the engine.' He made adjustments to their course and flicked the engine into neutral. To Kate, it appeared that they were still approaching the craggy stone jetty far too quickly and she looked at him in consternation.

'. . . and then we apply the brakes!'

He swung the anchor to and fro and then let it go. It splashed into the water behind them and he payed out the line.

To Kate's eye, the rough edge of the jetty was about to wreck them, but at the last minute the anchor rope tightened and they slowed. He walked nonchalantly past her and with one hand holding the bow rope, sprang ashore and swiftly tied them up.

She followed him up to the bow and leaned on the guard rail.

'I see you are well used to handling *Liberté* on your own,' she observed.

He grinned up at her. 'A little,' he replied and shrugged. 'But now, what about that swim? The other side of the jetty is best. You will find a little cove with a sandy beach. I will finish things here and then bring the sail board round if you would still like a lesson?'

'I would,' she said, pleased that he had remembered. 'Very much.'

Some minutes later found her standing in the shallows watching him skilfully sailing the surfer round from the jetty. She was refreshed, for the short swim through the clear water had been a delight.

'Conditions for learning are perfect,' he said as he came up to her. 'Hardly any waves and the landbreeze is still gentle.'

She was impatient, eager to try it out and he quickly explained the principles of the sailboard.

'You will find it takes a little time to get your balance,' he warned, but she had towed the board out and was clambering aboard.

She promptly fell off.

When she surfaced, spluttering and gasping, he was shaking with laughter, hands on his hips.

'You are too impetuous, Katherine,' he called. 'Come here, where you will still be in your depth and can get the basic things right first.'

A little chastened, she did as he suggested and gradually, with his patient help, she learned to bring her uncoordinated ankles into tune with the movements of the board and to use her weight correctly to haul the brightly coloured sail up out of the water. He helped her by holding the board steady.

At last she was standing upright, a little wobbly but nevertheless upright. He was holding the front of the board and smiling encouragement, his teeth white against the tan of his face.

'Now you are ready. Good. No, don't move suddenly,' he urged. 'Just lean back and pull the sail towards you and lean the mast forward. Slowly now. Do not stick your bottom out!'

Suddenly she was sailing. She caught a taste of how it really should be. It was like learning to ride a bicycle—that moment when the supporting hand was gone from your saddle and you were wobbling along on your own.

But not for long. She leaned back, over-confident. Too far—and again the blue water closed over her head. This time there were red and yellow colours as well, for when she surfaced she found she had pulled the sail over herself and she was beneath it. For a moment it was quite un-pleasant—a nasty, trapped sort of feeling. But it was only momentary, for the sail was suddenly whipped aside and Laurent's strong arm was round her, helping her regain her footing in the waist-deep water. His face was anxious.

'You are OK?' He was holding her—a hand on each of her hips. Her arms rested lightly on his.

'Yes, fine,' she laughed up at him. 'I was going well there for a little while, wasn't I?'

'Yes,' he said. 'For a *little* while!'

Their eyes met—and then the fun died in his, to be replaced by something different.

He pulled her to him fiercely and crushed his lips down upon hers, one arm sliding round her waist, the other caressing her bare back. Her lips parted in protestation and his tongue entered and explored her mouth. She could taste the salt on him, feel the firmness of his shoulders under her arms. He was pulling her urgently against him and slowly her protesting movements became those of response. Her mind began to spin dizzily as she felt his skin beneath her hands, wet and cool from the water. Despite herself, her fingers moved up to caress the back of his neck and she felt her pulse thumping. His mouth left hers and began to move sweetly down the curve of her neck. She could feel the wetness of his hair against her cheek, sense the hard strength of him pressing against her. Through half closed eyes she could see the sky, the sea, as if in a dream.

Suddenly he tensed, with a sharp intake of breath, followed almost immediately by an exasperated sort of sound.

He pushed her aside roughly, his attention on something behind her. She turned to see the wind surfer gently drifting out to sea, blown along by the off-shore breeze.

With a muttered curse, he plunged after it in a powerful crawl. He retrieved it and waded back towards her. She stood there, feeling strangely vulnerable and rejected. His eyes, still dark with passion, scrutinised her. She realised she was shivering, goose prickles on her bare skin. She knew that, with the cold, her nipples were clearly outlined through the thin material of the wet swimming costume. Concerned that he should think that this condition had some other cause, she folded her arms against her breasts and glared at him defiantly. His eyes returned her gaze.

'It's getting cold,' she asserted, determined to stare him out.

'Yes,' he said abruptly. 'I will sail back to *Liberté*. You will be able to find a way through from the beach.' He waved dismissively towards the shore and was gone, sliding up on to the wind surfer and pulling up the sail in a single movement.

Kate made her way back to the beach and through to the little stone jetty. She could not find a towel in the cabin so she seized a blanket from a side berth and flew into the rear cabin where she peeled off the swimsuit and dried herself vigorously. She was quite determined to be fully dressed by the time he returned.

CHAPTER EIGHT

SHE heard a thump as he brought the sail board alongside the hull. She had settled herself down in the main cabin with one of his nautical books, not so much because she wanted something to read, but more because she did not wish it to look as though she were waiting for him.

She knew she had not wanted the embrace out on the beach to end and she was puzzled and hurt at his behaviour. He had seemed angry afterwards—far more so than was warranted by having to swim after the wind surfer. That could only leave her as the cause of his irritation. He was such a creature of changing moods. She tried to focus her attention on the print of the book but she could still feel the pressure of his lips on hers, the strength of his encircling arms.

There was a series of bumps and slithering noises as he lashed the sail board down on the deck above her head. She realised that she was practically holding her breath and she concentrated on relaxing and regaining her composure. She swallowed, but her mouth had gone quite dry. This was ridiculous. She had been kissed many times—not on a romantic Greek shore perhaps, but never in a way she could not handle. She would have to keep this Frenchman at a distance—arms' length at least. She heard him jump down into the cockpit and a face appeared at the hatch.

To her amazement, all trace of his former ran-
cour had gone.

'Ah, there you are,' he observed, almost breezi-
ly. 'I'm ravenous. Swimming gives one an appetite,
n'est-ce pas?'

She nodded dumbly but he had not paused for
her reply and was chatting on. 'I will get dry and
change, then go and telephone Spiro.' He was in
the cabin now and his tall presence seemed to fill it.
He pulled a towel out of a locker and made his way
through to a cabin up in the bows. It was as if a
whirlwind had passed through.

She had certainly not been prepared for this
change of approach. She experienced a feeling of
mild resentment. Obviously it had been just a
casual clinch out there on the beach.

Well, she decided, her crew duties were certainly
not going to include being kissed whenever the
whims of the skipper dictated. She would concentrate on remaining aloof if they were going to spend
the evening together—not unfriendly of course,
but certainly not encouraging any more advances.
Anyway, she shrugged, Mary Jollison was bound to
be concerned about her being away overnight and
she would probably have to be driven back to
Netriti. When he returned from making the telephone call, however, and peered down into the
cabin grinning triumphantly with two thumbs
raised, her heart leaped with pleasure.

'All is well at Netriti,' he said. 'We will have a
pleasant evening, Katherine.' He swung down the
companionway steps. 'We can go whenever you are
ready. In fact it is almost dusk, now.'

'Well, I'll just go and slip back into a skirt. How
warm is it outside?'

'The land breeze has died now and it is a very red sunset. I have a feeling there will be no wind at all, tomorrow,' he replied, peering up at the sky through the open hatch. 'But certainly it is warm enough for a skirt I would say.' He paused. 'You can take the rear cabin to sleep in tonight, Katherine, so leave your things in there.'

'But I thought they were your quarters,' she hesitated. 'Where will you . . . ?'

'I am perfectly happy in a sleeping bag in the forecabin.' He shrugged. 'I cannot be bothered to make up bunks most of the time when I am aboard on my own. *Mon dieu*, all that business with sheets and blankets! But for a young lady, fresh linen and a pillow are important, *n'est-ce pas*?'

'I assure you I can rough it with the best of them if it is necessary,' she retorted and went through to change. Secretly though, she was relieved that the sleeping arrangements had been made clear. She did not want there to be any misunderstandings. Now she could look forward to the pleasure of dinner in a Greek taverna without any qualms as to what might be expected of her later. It *would* be an enjoyable evening.

In fact, it was a delightful evening. Laurent and Stavros, the owner of the taverna, were apparently old friends and she was warmly included in the shared greetings, which also involved meeting Stavros's wife and eldest daughter, a perfectly charming young sixteen year-old.

The air was balmy and the setting delightful. The taverna was small and set back from the harbour, with tables out in the open air under a vine-covered pergola. She waited expectantly for Stavros to show them to their seats, but to her surprise, he was beckoning them into the kitchen at the back. Surely they were not going to have their meal with the family.

'We go to choose our food from the kitchen,' Laurent explained, seeing her puzzlement. 'It is the custom.'

They made their way through to where Stavros was proudly displaying various dishes.

'Would you like some fish, Katherine?' asked Laurent. 'These are delicious. They are like sea bass and Stavros's wife cooks them over a charcoal grill.' Seeing her smile of agreement, he went on, 'We could have a smallish one each—or this big one shared between us. That would be more fun, I think, and the flavour of the big one will be better.'

'Whatever you say, Laurent,' she replied. 'We used to have a lot of fish in Devon, fresh from the Salcombe fishermen. You could taste the sea.'

'Here also,' he laughed. 'You will see. Perhaps an assortment of your specialities as an hors d'oeuvre, eh Stavros? And a Greek salad with fetta cheese. And a bottle of Kolossi, I think.'

Stavros's English was quite good and, with everything settled, they were led to their table, looking out over a sea which was now cloaked in velvety darkness.

Any misgivings she had about him completely dissipated as the meal progressed. To start with, they were brought a mixture of delicacies which Laurent insisted she try in turn. There were delicious little helpings of seasoned rice wrapped in vine leaves, which Stavros called dolmadakia and a dish of tiny shrimps and mushrooms cooked in a wine sauce. There was taramasalata too, which Kate had tasted before, but never with the flavour that Stavros had achieved.

The high point was the sea bass, brought to them by Stavros's daughter. The girl was very aware of Laurent and painfully shy, hardly raising her eyes to acknowledge their thanks. He seemed unaware of the effect he had on her, however, and launched into a careful demonstration to Kate of how to dissect the fish and avoid the bones. It lay on a plate between them, garnished with parsley, lemon and rigani herbs. His face reflected his concentration as he wielded the knife and fork, serving delicious pieces across to her plate. He sensed her eyes upon him and looked up, catching her gaze. Her heart jolted as he smiled.

To finish with, they were brought delicate little confections of flaky pastry filled with almonds and honey. They sat back in their chairs, replete, and there was an air of relaxed companionship.

'Do you think you will always live in Corfu now?' she asked.

'I am not sure,' he replied. 'It is practically my home, I think. Certainly, the work is more worth-while. I was not happy in Paris, you know. For a few years it was a good life there but then things went wrong and I came to Greece. But I don't know if I will stay.'

'You came here to escape from the pressures of life in Paris?'

'Yes. And from other things.' His face was partly in shadow and although she wanted to ask more, to understand him better, she refrained, for she sensed a shutter descending on the conversation and she was fearful of breaking the magic of the evening. She pulled her cardigan up over her shoulders.

'You are not cold, Katherine?' He leaned forward anxiously.

'No, not at all, thank you, Laurent. Everything is just lovely.' Her hand was resting on the table and for a split second she had the certain conviction that he was going to reach across and take it in his. But the moment passed.

Then, above the gentle lap of water on the shore and the buzz of crickets, she heard a new sound. It was a short note, soft and haunting, like a child calling the letter 'Q' in a very high treble. She waited and it came again, floating out from the darkness of the pines on the hillside behind the taverna. She cocked her head on one side listening and saw that he did the same.

'It is a skops owl,' he said quietly. 'You will hear others in a short while.' They sat listening and soon a second 'Q' came across the bay. At first she thought it was an echo of the first, but the sounds were not in unison and sometimes coincided, sometimes were apart. Then there was a third call—and a fourth. The sounds seemed to circle them where they sat alone in the pool of light under the pergola.

He was smiling gently.

'The skops are tiny birds, almost too small to produce sounds of such intensity.' He paused. 'Some say they are really the spirits of dead Greek warriors, calling for the maidens whom they loved on the night before battle. They say that the hills around Thermopylae, where a handful of Greeks fought against the Spartan hordes, are alive with the sound of their calling.'

Kate nodded as if in a spell and then shivered and rubbed her bare arms.

'You do not like the story?' he asked.

'Oh I do. It's just that it sounds rather sad.'

'Perhaps so.'

They lapsed back into silence.

A voice came from behind her and she turned, startled, for she had not heard Stavros approach.

'It will be calm tomorrow, I think, Laurent.' Stavros came into the circle of light, a tray tucked under his arm. 'Always it is a calm day when the skops come and call to us from the pine trees,' he explained, smiling at Kate. 'You enjoyed the fish I hope?'

'It was delicious,' she said. 'It was a fine fish.'

'And he had a noble end,' said Stavros, 'to be enjoyed by two such as yourself and Laurent. And now, some more coffee?'

'No, Stavros, thank you. We have had a long day and some good sailing. I think Miss Trelawney must be tired.' Seeing her nod of assent, he added, 'I will come through and pay you.'

They walked back to the jetty along the beach and she marvelled again at the beauty of the place—the silent hills, their features shadowed by the moonlight, the tall pines standing like sentinels along the ridges and always the quiet sea. The plaintive 'Q's' of the skops owls still drifted down from the trees.

He took her hand to help her climb up the steps to the jetty, his grasp cool and firm. They reached the top of the wall and she made no move to disengage her hand. Nor did he. They walked along the jetty towards the Swan and she could feel her heart beating, hoping and hoping that he would stop, turn and take her in his arms.

But they reached the boat and each needed both

hands to climb aboard. Down in the cabin he fumbled for the light switch and turned to her.

'I hope you will be comfortable, Katherine,' he said gruffly.

'I'm sure I will be,' she replied. 'And you, Laurent, you will be OK in the forecabin?'

There was a silence. She knew that if she prolonged this moment a minute longer he would reach for her, that the decision was hers alone and that if he kissed her again, there would be no turning back.

'Well, goodnight, Laurent,' she blurted. He was staring at her and she dragged her eyes from his gaze. At her cabin door she summoned the will to turn and face him again.

'It was a charming evening. Thank you.'

He said nothing, but continued to stare at her. She could feel his eyes boring into her, even after she pushed her cabin door shut behind her and leaned back against it, her knees weak and her heart beating wildly.

There was a tiny washroom off the cabin and she prepared for bed in a daze. She always carried a little travelling toothbrush with her, but realised that she had not of course brought any nightclothes.

She slipped into the bunk, the crisp sheets cool on her nakedness and stared at the cabin roof, lit dimly in the moonlight which reflected in from the portholes. She could hear him moving around in the main saloon and a thud as he pulled the deck hatch shut. Then there was a silence. She could just make out her cabin door and the gleam of its brass handle. For a moment she was convinced it was turning, that he was coming to her. But the silence prevailed. The beating of her heart slowed and she was alone with the gentle creak of the ship and the lap of the water outside on the hull.

She fell into a fitful sleep, troubled with dreams of a tall figure bending over her, of strong arms tenderly holding her and words breathed softly in her ear. She knew that she had never felt like this. Words of endearment never really meant before were rising to her lips. She awoke several times to find her bedclothes in disarray and his name uppermost in her mind, being murmured over and over . . .

An insistent knocking on a door penetrated her consciousness.

'Katherine, Katherine. Are you awake? I have made the English cup of tea for Sunday morning. You would like me to bring you one?'

'Oh, yes please,' she called out and then, fully awake, remembered that she was not wearing a nightie and hurriedly drew the bedclothes up to her neck.

She heard a chivalrously slow fumbling with the door handle and then it opened and a hand holding a steaming mug appeared.

He cleared his throat. 'You are decent?' he enquired.

'Oh, er, yes,' she stammered. Good heavens, she could feel a pink blush in her cheeks. She snuggled down and pulled the sheets up under her nose. He came in and put the mug down within easy reach on a side locker.

'There is absolutely no wind, nor likely to be,' he grinned down at her ruefully. 'I have rung the airport in Corfu and the forecast is for a flat calm.

We will have to leave *Liberté* here and complete our journey across the island by car. I have already rung Spiro and he will be here by eleven.'

'Oh, I see.'

The disappointment in her voice must have been acutely apparent for he added, 'We will have a proper sail another time, perhaps. And now, I will cook breakfast. I have bought eggs and bread from Stavros at the taverna.' He disappeared through to the saloon and she heard the clatter of pans in the galley.

The morning passed all too quickly. It seemed that they had only just finished breakfast, expertly prepared by Laurent and eaten out on the deck in the warm sun, when they heard the toot of a car horn and the big Peugeot came into view on the road leading down to the jetty. A grinning Stavros appeared, coming towards them with his familiar rolling gait.

All too soon they were reabsorbed into the land-bound world. It seemed that she had been away from the Villa Netriti for ages, but it was barely twenty-four hours since she had met Laurent at the ferry terminal.

They dropped him off at his apartment in Corfu and she had the impression that he had plans for his Sunday afternoon.

She felt a strong sense of anti-climax as they drew away and took the road to Netriti.

CHAPTER NINE

THE feelings of restlessness and anti-climax on her return to the villa persisted as the days passed. The memories of their trip together and the dinner at Petrossos filled her every thought. Nor was she able to immerse herself in her nursing routine, for Paul Jollison was recovering in leaps and bounds. He was now able to walk all the way to the cliff top without his walking stick. He still wanted it to be taken but Kate insisted that it was carried by whoever was accompanying him.

Gradually she realised that her days on this beautiful island were numbered, for her nursing assignment was coming closer to its end with each fresh step Paul Jollison took. She would not admit to herself that she had already fallen deeply in love with Laurent and that it was the pain of probably never seeing him again after she had left that was really distressing her. He was merely a very attractive and extremely independent man, given to superficial relationships—and very much an established bachelor, she told herself. Moreover, she knew absolutely nothing about him other than that he had some mysterious past in Paris. He was a skilled doctor though, and a dedicated one. She could understand his impatience with the imagined ills of rich city-dwellers. No, Laurent de Kerouac was just someone who shared her enjoyment of sailing and that was all there could ever be to it. And anyway, he had probably been sailing with hundreds of girls, she thought sadly.

This was brought home to her one morning when Madeleine turned up. Kate had woken with a pleasant feeling of anticipation, for it was the day for Laurent's mid-week visit. The sound of the girl's battered motor scooter and the sight of it parked in the courtyard were distinctly unwelcome. Her half-hearted offers to help with the language problems had been followed up with equally half-hearted visits and she had only reappeared on two or three occasions. When she had come, she seemed more interested in lolling around in the kitchen, gossiping with Spiro, than enquiring whether Kate needed any help. Today however she seemed unusually inquisitive and greeted Kate with something approaching interest.

'I hear you've been on a sailing trip?' she enquired, eyeing Kate with bored disdain.

'Yes, I have,' replied Kate, matching the girl's tone and surprised at her own reaction. 'It was very enjoyable.'

'I'm sure. Pity it was so short. I gather the wind died on you and you had to leave the boat at Petrossos?' Madeleine was leaning arrogantly against the kitchen table, idly inspecting her nails. Kate muttered an affirmative and went to the sink to deposit the cup from her previous night's bedtime drink. Madeleine seemed very well informed, she reflected resentfully.

'Of course,' added the girl, 'he'll ask me to help him sail the boat back from Petrossos. In fact I would have crewed on the leg from Paxos, but he knows I'm busy with yacht charters. It's the start of the season and Giles Stephens finds it difficult to spare me.'

'I'm sure you're absolutely indispensable,' said Kate with heavy sarcasm. The girl did not seem to notice the dangerous note in Kate's voice and was now inspecting the nails on the other hand.

'I expect he told you about his life in Paris?' she went on. 'He'll never settle down you know. That's why he came to Corfu in the first place. Always on the move. Still I expect he told you his life's history over dinner. At Stavros's taverna was it?'

Kate turned on her, the anger welling up which she was trying frantically to contain.

'As a matter of fact, he did not tell me his life's history,' she snapped. 'Probably because I am not in the habit of asking personal questions about other people's private affairs. Now, if there is no further information that I can give you, I will wish you good morning.' She paused at the door. 'Oh, and I'm finding the phrase book you gave me surprisingly useful. In fact it's so surprisingly useful that I think I will be able to do without any further visits from you.' Mustering her utmost dignity, she stalked back to her room.

Of course she knew he would never settle down. But what he did was of no concern to her. He had probably had dozens of love affairs. She heard the clatter of the Madeleine girl's motor scooter starting up outside. He probably thought that she, Kate, was fairly unexciting. No, she was certainly not his type, nor was it of any consequence either, she tried to tell herself.

She felt very close to tears. She could feel their hot prickle behind her eyes. Why had she let Madeleine upset her like that? She was normally very much in control of herself, but that creature's

condescending manner and obviously far deeper
knowledge of his background had really provoked
her. What on earth did he see in the girl? She was
no more than a very self-centred adolescent—and
an extremely young one as well. It was probably her
rather obvious female attributes that attracted him,
she thought.

After breakfast, she wandered round the villa,
but there was not a great deal to occupy her. Mary
and Paul were comfortably ensconced in armchairs
on the verandah, reading. She chatted with them
for a while. It was not even necessary to supervise
Paul's exercises now, for she had developed a
programme for him that he was quite capable of
doing on his own—and so he should, for it helped
his self-sufficiency even more.

'Why don't you go for a swim, dear?' said Mary,
vaguely aware that Kate was restless.

'I think I will. I might even go and beg some fruit
and cheese from Elena and take some lunch and my
book,' she replied.

She spent a pleasant few hours of total self-
indulgence down by the sea. After that first dis-
astrous sunbathing excursion, she had found an
even more secluded spot—no more than a hollow
in the rocks, but hidden from view on all sides. She
had made this her base and encouraged by the
security it provided, daily left her bikini top off for
longer and longer periods.

Today she left it off for several hours and stretched herself out, soaking up the sun in great waves
until its penetrating warmth produced the most
delicious languor in her body and limbs. Determined that she would be back in plenty of time for
his visit, she had plunged into the clear water for a

swim around mid-afternoon and refreshed, made her way back to the villa, pleased at the prospect of seeing him.

A short time before he was due, however, there was a knock at her door and she opened it to find Spiro standing there. The doctor was on the 'phone and wished to speak with her, he said.

She sped over to the kitchen and grasped the receiver dangling on the end of its cord.

'Katherine, I will not be coming today. There is a lot to do here in the surgery and I have had two emergency calls this morning. I am very behind.'

'Oh yes, of course,' she replied lightly, although she knew she was disappointed. 'It's all right. Everything's fine here.'

'Mr Jollison is doing well?'

'Yes, very well. I would say he's well enough now to go out on an excursion. Mary's been going on about buying presents to take back with them.'

'Well, I think a little trip out would be a good idea. Why not ask Spiro to drive you on a shopping expedition tomorrow?'

'Yes, I suppose we could. It would do them both good.'

There was a silence.

'When will I see . . . I mean when will you be coming next?'

'I'm not sure, Katherine. I have a lot of personal affairs to resolve at present. But you can always ring me if there's a problem.'

'Yes, of course.'

'Well, I must go. Goodbye, Katherine.'

'Yes. Goodbye, Laurent.'

She put the 'phone down, feeling very empty. It was as though the sun she had been basking in

earlier had suddenly gone behind clouds. She
shrugged and telling herself to stop behaving so
foolishly, went in search of the Jollisons.

Mary was very excited at the prospect of a shopping trip. 'I think Spiro said there's a market in
Corfu Town on Friday. It's not one of his days at
the yacht charter company, is it?'

'No, I don't think so. I'll go and arrange things
now,' replied Kate. 'He can drive us down there for
a few hours. We might even have lunch out.'

And so it was that Friday morning found them
walking through the narrow streets of Corfu Town.
It was a colourful place and they were soon immersed in present buying. Or at least, Mary was.
She had a long list, which she kept consulting over
with Paul. Kate did not join in, deciding that she
would prefer to come in again on her own.

Although it was only May, the town was crowded
with tourists. As they entered one of the market
streets, with its collection of stalls and eager shop-
pers, Kate became concerned that the constant
jostling would tire Paul.

'I think we should take a breather and have a cup
of coffee. We don't want to overdo things,' she
declared firmly and taking his arm, led them in
amongst the tables of an outdoor cafe. They settled
down under a large sun umbrella.

Kate ordered the coffees and they relaxed in the
comfortable wicker chairs, watching the passing
crowd and busy market traders. Their table was in a
little backwater, still part of the atmosphere but
well out of the mainstream. Her eyes strayed over a
stall selling embroidered Greek linen and dresses.
The colours were beautiful and the flowing cotton
looked cool in the sunlight. A dark haired girl was

reaching up and taking down a dress from the hanging display. There was something familiar about her—and about the set of her companion's shoulders.

She realised she was looking at Madeleine and the doctor. She reached out an arm to attract Mary and Paul's attention, but something stopped her and she sat back watching.

Madeleine held the dress up against herself, emphasising her figure by holding it in against her waist with the other hand. Kate could not help lip reading the 'What do you think?' as the girl smiled coyly up at Laurent, her head tilted to one side.

Laurent stood back and then obviously asked a question about the length, for Madeleine lifted a leg forward and peered down. He asked another question and she nodded vigorously. It was a lovely dress, very simple in plain cotton, with a low-cut flowing neckline. Madeleine would look sensational in it, thought Kate, her emotions in a turmoil.

She watched Laurent reach in his back pocket and pass a wad of drachmae to the stall owner, who took the dress, swiftly wrapped it and gave it to Madeleine. She slipped an arm round Laurent's waist and hugged him, standing on tip-toe to kiss him on the cheek. Arm in arm, they disappeared into the crowd and with them went Kate's enjoyment of the day.

Fortunately, Mary was too engaged in her own plans to notice Kate's cheerlessness, but she felt Paul's eye on her, especially at lunch, when she ate little. She had a glass of wine however, which sent her into a doze on the return journey in the car. She needed hardly any encouragement to have a siesta when they got back to Netriti and she curled up on her bed and soon dropped off. Dimly she became aware of a gentle tapping on her door.

'Are you awake, dear?'

'Yes, Mary,' she called. 'What is it?'

'We wondered if you would like a cup of tea. Dr de Kerouac's here.'

Kate blinked into wakefulness. It was not a dream then. She had half heard his car as she dozed but had vaguely thought it was one of those peculiar dream impressions mid-way between sleep and wakefulness.

She splashed some cold water on her face from the basin in the corner, quickly repaired what little makeup she was wearing and ran a brush through her hair. She hesitated and then applied a touch of her favourite perfume to the inside of her wrists.

The three of them were sitting comfortably round a table outside, quietly chatting.

'Ah *bonjour* sleepyhead,' grinned Laurent, rising to his feet and pulling a chair out for her. Mary poured her a cup of tea.

'Paul and Mary have been telling me about your shopping expedition this morning. Another big step forward for our patient.'

'Yes indeed, Dr de Kerouac,' she replied in a very formal tone without looking at him. She did not see the fleeting look of puzzlement on his face.

'And you visited the market, I hear. I was there myself. We might have bumped into each other.'

We practically did, thought Kate miserably, but you were too busy buying dresses for your girl-friend to notice.

There was a silence.

'Well anyway, Kate, Dr de Kerouac has been

anxiously wanting to know if we can spare you to him for the whole weekend. We've assured him that of course we can,' announced Mary.

Kate's eyes opened in consternation. 'Oh, but I—' she stammered.

'I wish I was coming, I can tell you,' interjected Paul. 'It sounds a lovely trip.'

'Never mind, dear, we can see the other side of the island by road. Now that you are declared fit to get out and about, we must take more advantage of the car and Spiro,' said Mary.

Kate realised that they were all three regarding her, expectant smiles on their faces.

'You will come, Katherine, won't you?' Laurent was looking at her anxiously. 'I thought we'd take *Liberté* down the coast and up the other side of Corfu, perhaps visit the islands off the North Coast. Spiro can drive us down to Petrossos early tomorrow and we needn't come back until Monday.'

'It'll be lovely,' said Mary.

'Fabulous,' said Paul.

This was impossible. She could not refuse without appearing foolish. After all, she could give no reason.

'She talked about nothing else after your last trip,' said Paul, stirring his tea.

'I er, well thank you,' she mumbled and then, almost defiantly, 'what about your regular crew?'

He stared at her in puzzlement.

'But I don't have a regular crew. I sail on my own mostly. I told you.'

Good heavens, he almost looked hurt.

A voice which she could not possibly believe was her own said, 'I'd love to come.'

From that point on, everything became rather

unreal. She could not imagine what had possessed her to accept his invitation. Why, only that morning she had seen him in the company of a very attractive young lady with whom he obviously had an intimate relationship. Now she, Kate, was agreeing to spend a weekend with him.

But she knew how to look after herself, she reasoned. She had handled difficult situations before and he had behaved impeccably on the last night they had been aboard together. Anyway, she was keeping him at arms' length from now on.

Caught up with everyone's enthusiasm for the trip, she felt a rising wave of excitement. The chance to sail a *Nautor Swan* around the beautiful Ionian sea was rare indeed and their last trip together had been heaven. How stupid to behave like some moody schoolgirl.

'What about provisions and things,' she exclaimed.

'I'll ring through to Stavros and he'll let us have some fresh things from the taverna in the morning,' replied Laurent. 'There's plenty of non-perishables on board already, coffee, tea and so forth. All you've got to do is turn up. Do you fancy an early start? You and Spiro pick me up at seven?'

'Why not?' she said gaily.

And so it was settled.

A cheerful Spiro deposited them and their bags on the jetty at Petrossos early next morning and they clambered aboard. There was a pleasantly familiar feel about the *Swan*, she thought, as she dumped her bag in the rear cabin and went back through to the main saloon.

'I will go and fetch the provisions from Stavros,'

he said, 'and then we can be off.' He pulled out a chart of Corfu. 'I thought we'd sail back down the South Corfu Channel and round the other side. It's a more exposed coast, so there are more interesting bays. In places you can anchor in shelter and explore.' He grinned. 'Ever done any skin diving?'

'A little,' she replied. 'But only in Devon, never in water as clear as here.'

'Then you're in for a treat. Have a look at the chart while I go across to the taverna.' He swung up the companionway steps.

'I could be sorting out the sails,' she called up after him.

His face reappeared.

'OK,' he said and peered up at the sky. 'What do you think? The wind's quite fresh this morning.'

'Mainsail and Number One headsail?' she suggested.

'Agreed,' he said and was gone.

By the time he came back, carrying the box of provisions she had practically got the boat ready.

Soon they were heading out of Petrossos, bound South. The day was brilliantly clear and they could easily see the coast of mainland Greece over and away to the East.

He moved around, hauling a rope here and there and they heeled to the wind. She could feel the boat come alive and she went and stood on the cabin roof, one arm round the stays supporting the mast.

'Some sailing, eh?' His shout of jubilation reached her and she turned to nod vigorously. He was standing by the wheel, one foot on the side locker, balancing himself effortlessly against the driving surge of the *Swan's* progress. Their wake streamed out behind him, boiling and flashing in the sunlight like a straight white furrow across a rolling blue meadow. Up ahead, the spray began to fly in great glistening arcs.

He lifted his head and laughed with the exhilaration of it, the sound carrying away in the wind. His mood was infectious and she caught it, turning her face into the wind and letting it blow back the fair hair from her face. She could still smell the scent of the pinewoods borne down to them from the shore.

By midday they were well down the South Corfu Channel and *Liberté* was practically sailing herself in the fresh breeze. Kate had busied herself in the galley and passed him up sandwiches and coffee. She joined him in the cockpit, carrying her own mug. He made room for her.

'You are used to balancing yourself in the galley of a heeling ship, I see,' he observed and she nodded.

'We get some pretty strong blows in the English Channel,' she replied. She knew she was enjoying herself as she had never done before. She did not care about his past, whatever it might have been, or Madeleine or anything. It was good just to be in his company, sharing something they both loved.

'Sometimes it blows hard here, too,' he said. 'Quite often when conditions seem at their clearest. Like today. We will have to keep an eye on the weather.' She looked around in puzzlement. She could scarcely believe conditions could be better. The sky was clear with not a sign of cloud.

By the time they reached the southern tip of Corfu, however, it was clear that the wind strength had increased. *Liberté* was heeling over much more and the seas seemed bigger.

'I think perhaps we will change to a smaller

headsail before we turn the corner and head up the West Coast,' he said.

'Shall I get it?' she asked.

'No. You steer and I will do it. You are OK to handle her?'

'Yes, I think so.'

He moved aside and let her take the wheel. He waited to see that she was comfortably in control of the big yacht and then went down to the sail locker.

She braced herself against the pull of the wheel. He had made the right decision, she realised, for *Liberté* was straining against the thrust of the wind, like an impetuous animal on its leash. She watched with some relief as Laurent reappeared, carrying a sailbag and made his way up front. He grinned at her as he passed and it was obvious he was revelling in the conditions. He deftly untied ropes and the headsail slithered to the deck in a flapping, crackling flurry of canvas. The effect was immediate for as *Liberté* was relieved of some of the press of her sails, her violent motion eased. He clipped on the smaller sail and hoisted it.

'That's better,' he said as he rejoined her at the wheel. 'But perhaps when we turn the tip of Corfu it will be windier still.' He looked at her. 'You do not mind if it blows a little?'

'No, not a bit. Now that we have reduced sail, it is better. I enjoy it. She is a good boat.'

He nodded, satisfied, and they lapsed into a companionable silence as the *Swan* ploughed her way down to the headland. Now and again, they ran into a larger wave and the spray flew higher. She felt the spatter of it on her cheek.

'I think we may need sailing waterproofs. I will

fetch them—I have a spare for you,' he said. 'And we should really be wearing safety harnesses.'

He returned and took the wheel as she slipped the bright yellow anorak over her head. She dropped the harness and its lifeline in a side locker for the moment however—it would restrict her movements and Laurent was not wearing his yet. His attention was now completely on the boat and the wind, head tilted back, eyes checking the line of the sail, the run of their course. The big steering wheel seemed much smaller in his hands than hers and he piloted the *Swan* with sensitive skill, now letting her have her head, now checking her, as they ran on through the glittering water.

Eventually they reached the tip of the headland and began to round it. The sea here was a very different sight, for out of the shelter of the island there was a mass of white horses moving in towards them. They came hard on the wind and began to pound through the seas, the *Swan* slicing great swathes through the water.

She noticed that during the activity of turning the headland and adjusting ropes, the sun had slipped behind clouds. The change in the sea's mood was noticeable, for without the sun's reflection it had gone a dull, leaden sort of colour and its character had become distinctly unfriendly.

They plunged on for a while and then he turned to her.

'I think perhaps we should change our plans. On this course we are simply sailing into bad weather and it would not be prudent to be caught on a difficult shore with a strong wind from the West like this.'

She shouted agreement, noticing that it was now

necessary to lift her voice above the rising wind.

'Whatever you think, Laurent.'

'There is a haven over on the mainland, a sheltered spot between two islets. I think we are in for a
real Mediterranean storm and we can ride it out
there quite comfortably. I am sorry, you will miss
your skin diving.'

'It doesn't matter,' she shouted. 'It is better to be
sensible.'

His eyes shone for a moment as he appreciated
her agreement.

'*Bien*, we will turn then,' he decided and spun the
wheel. The yacht slewed and began to run down
before the wind. The seas into which they had
been pounding now began to chase them, lifting
Liberté's stern high so that she began a wild
cork-screwing motion. It was like riding a roller-
coaster.

'I think that we still have too much sail up. I will
take some reefs into the mainsail as well. Can you
take the wheel again?'

She watched him working up by the mast,
fighting the sails. Now and then he looked back at
her, grinning as he won his battle with the wind, his
teeth flashing as white as the flying spray.

He almost seemed part of the storm itself.

It was really very rough now, she thought, catching a glimpse of a large sea coming up behind them,
its crest breaking with a hiss. Still, she had been out
in worse weather conditions with her father and
brother in the family's ketch and Laurent was
obviously a good seaman. You just had to keep
your head, she told herself.

He was gesticulating at her to haul on a rope and
she reached over for it. It was just beyond her

grasp. She changed her position and stood up, holding on to the wheel with one hand and reaching out with other.

'*Prenez-garde!*'

His shouted warning came a split second too late, for the deck rose like an express lift as an enormous sea hit *Liberté's* stern and Kate's grip on the wheel was lost. She made a frantic grab for the guard rails, but they swung away from her tauntingly. She felt herself suspended in mid air.

'Laurent,' she screamed as she catapulted into the air and water and foam closed over her head.

For what seemed ages she just seemed to be going down and down. Then she felt herself straighten and she instinctively fought her way to the surface. She came up, gulping down air, spluttering and choking. She looked around, panic-stricken, and saw *Liberté* climbing up the slope of a wave, yards away. She caught a glimpse of Laurent at the stern. He was feverishly unclipping a lifebelt from the guard rail and he stood up and hurled it at her. She floundered towards it and grabbed at its reassuring buoyancy.

'Hold on, Katherine. I am coming back.' She could barely hear his words against the wind. She looked back and saw to her horror that *Liberté* had now completely disappeared. She could not even see her mast. She knew she was very, very frightened, for she had read many accounts of people falling overboard from sailing yachts. Everything depended on the skill of the person left behind at the wheel. Down here in the water, she knew she was almost invisible, especially in the troughs between the waves. Laurent would only be able to see her when she and *Liberté* were both on crests at the

same time. To find her he would have to sail back
on exactly the opposite course to that which they
had been holding. And he would be coming against
the wind. What a fool she had been not to clip on
her harness and lifeline as Laurent had suggested
and her father had drummed into her countless
times.

She shifted her grip on the lifebelt, willing herself
not to panic, telling herself to save her strength.

There. She caught a glimpse of a mast head, but
it was immediately hidden again behind a breaking
wave crest. It was hopeless, he would never be able
to find her. No, there it was again. A full glimpse of
the *Swan* that time. She lifted an arm and waved,
shouting his name, but the wind contemptuously
dashed the words from her mouth. She fought to
maintain her self-control. Use the whistle on the
life belt, a voice inside told her. Of course. She
snatched it from its holder and began blowing
short, urgent blasts. On the next crest she could see
that he had altered course and was lifting an arm in
acknowledgement.

In slow motion she watched the *Swan* closing the
distance which separated them. A rope loop came
snaking across the water.

'Slip it over your head and under your arms,' he
shouted.

It took every last ounce of her courage to aban-
don the safety of the lifebelt and grab the rope.
Then, as she felt the strength of the rope and the
pull as he hauled her towards the yacht, she knew
she was going to be all right. A wave bumped her
against the side and strong arms reached down for
her. She got a foot on the boarding ladder and
with failing strength pushed upwards. He pulled

her inboard and on to the bench seat in the cockpit.

His face was agonised, his hand futilely trying to brush away the hair plastered to her cheeks. She looked up at him.

'Oh Laurent,' she sobbed and threw her arms round his neck as though he represented life itself. He pulled her to him and buried her head in his shoulder.

'It's all right, it's all right now, *ma petite*.' His voice was in her ear.

'Oh Laurent, I was so frightened.'

'And I, Katherine. I thought I had lost you, my love.'

Suddenly she wanted nothing else but to feel his lips on hers. Their mouths met in a searing, urgent fusing of need. They clung together and it was as if the storm abated momentarily, for there was just him and the strength of his arms. She felt her body stirring.

Then it was over and they broke apart, staring at each other, shocked at the intensity of their emotions.

'Come, Katherine. You must change out of those clothes.' He was shouting over the shriek of the wind. Untended, *Liberté* was drifting on the sea, her mast tracing crazy figures of eight on the stormy sky. If anything, the sea was rougher.

'You must go below and get warm,' he cried and she nodded, realising that she was shaking uncontrollably, her teeth chattering.

'Can you manage?' he asked. 'I must stay on the helm.'

'Yes, I can manage. And you, you will be all right up here on your own?' she shouted.

'Of course. We have two, maybe three hours o
this and then we will be under the lee of the island
at Sivota. Now you must go below.'

She made her way precariously across the pitch
ing cockpit and down below into the saloon.

Down here was relative tranquillity. She swung
herself from handrail to handrail into the rear cabin
and braced herself against the bunk. With numbed
fingers she tugged off the waterproofs, shedding
pools of water everywhere, and searched in her bag
for the large beach towel she had brought. Sodden
items of clothing followed one another on to the
cabin floor until she was naked, briskly trying to rub
some circulation back into her trembling body.

With most of the water removed, she grabbed a
blanket and swathing herself in it, fell exhausted on
the bunk.

The angle of the boat was such that she was
comfortably wedged in and gradually the trembling
eased and she began to relax. The texture of the
blanket was rough on her skin, but it was comforting. She felt warmth stealing back into her frozen
body. She drew her knees up to her chin and curled
into a ball, pulling a pillow under her head.

Above her, she could hear the fury of the storm
but from down here it seemed strangely muted.
Now and again, *Liberté* fell off the crest of a wave
with a tremendous, lurching crash and she could
hear the rattle of blocks and spars and the slash of
driven spray across the deck.

She drifted into a sort of limbo, assailed with
recollections of tumbling waves forming a background to Laurent as she had left him, wrestling
with the wheel, his lips drawn back in a snarl of
defiance at the storm. Now and again she thought

he heard snatches of the Marseillaise, sung in a
eep baritone . . .

ome time later, she emerged from under the
illow which she had grabbed to blot out the fury of
he storm to find that the cabin was in relative
wilight. *Liberté* was at rest, the terrible pitching
nd tumbling at an end, although the yacht was still
obbing and curtseying to the wind. But her motion
as checked somehow. They were at anchor, she
ealised and the yacht was gently snubbing at her
hain. She heard noises from the main saloon.

'Laurent?' she called and heard the thump of his
ea boots approaching her cabin door. It opened
nd a head appeared, wearing a cheerful grin. He
ad changed into a rough, navy blue rollneck swea-
er and his hair was a mass of shaggy curls where the
alt water had soaked it.

'So, the crew is awake. About time too. And how
o you feel, Katherine?'

'I'm fine now, thank you. Where are we?'

'In a little bay, tucked in behind the islands at
ivota. Quite safe now. Perhaps I will put out
nother anchor if the wind shifts, but we can easily
ide out the storm here.'

'I'm sorry I wasn't awake to help you bring us in,
aurent.'

'*Ça ne fait rien,*' he said. 'But now some food,
es? I am concocting one of my famous stews. Out
f cans mostly, not exactly French cuisine, but you
 will enjoy it, I hope.'

'It sounds wonderful,' she said. 'I will get up—'

'I would not hear of it,' he interrupted. 'You
ave had a bad fright. You must keep warm.'
Without waiting for a reply, he disappeared.

She pulled the blanket up more snugly under he
chin. His words had momentarily brought back th
horror she had felt as the sea closed over her hea
He had saved her life, for certain, this strange ma
of conflicting moods. His skill as a doctor wa
superceded by his skill as a seaman. She hoped h
did not think she was too foolish in so stupid
falling overboard.

She sat up and rummaged in her bag for the thic
woolly spare sweater she had brought and slipped
over her head. She sat back in the corner and pulle
the blanket up round her midriff. She was ver
hungry indeed and eagerly replied to his knock o
her door a few minutes later.

He came in, flicking on the cabin light and carry
ing a tray on which rested a steaming bowl. H
stood over her, smiling down.

'I will value your opinion on my cooking,' h
announced.

'But where is yours? Do bring it in here and eat
with me,' she insisted and he inclined his hea
graciously.

'That would be very pleasant.'

Together, they devoured the food like starvin
castaways, he perched on one end of the bunk, sh
curled up at the other. The stew was delicious an
she told him so.

They finished and he collected the plates, pu
ting them both on the locker top opposite. He sa
down again and gazed at her. She lowered he
eyes.

'Laurent, I don't know how to say it. You save
my life, you know, and I was so frightened. I don
know how to thank you. It was so silly just to fall i
like that. My father's always warned me of th

anger. You must think I'm an awful fool.' The
words came out in a rush and were only stilled when
e reached a hand out and placed a finger on her
ps. She raised her eyes to meet his.

Suddenly, he reached forward and gathered her
o him. She knew that it was going to happen and
he responded immediately, her arms going up and
round him. Their lips melted together in a kiss of
uch tenderness that her senses swam. She leaned
ack, pulling him down to her, his curls still damp
eneath the light touch of her fingers.

She felt his hand slide up the skin of her back
eneath the sweater. Then his caresses were be-
oming more insistent and she felt them move
ound to cup her gently swelling breasts, bare
eneath the rough wool. His fingers teased her
ipples. He was pushing the sweater upwards, his
ands stroking the soft curves of her body. He was
ooking at her and her heart desperately wanted
im to find her attractive. She suddenly felt very
hy.

'Katherine, Katherine.' The words were
reathed in her ear as he leaned forward again to
rush the side of her neck with his mouth. She
wisted and turned beneath him.

'Oh Laurent, I don't know. Laurent, please, I've
ever—'

He had moved his lips down across her bosom,
he sweater up under her arms, and was placing
urning kisses across her body. She could feel the
ard strength of him against her.

The edge of the blanket began to slide down
cross her stomach, the caress of his hand gentle
pon her hip. Her mind was a vortex of emotions.
he knew she did not want him to stop, that she

wanted to surrender to him, to let him make love t
her—

A harsh, grating sound filled the cabin and h
head came up, senses straining. The sound cam
again and he leaped to his feet.

'The anchor,' he shouted and rushed from th
cabin.

She fell back, her senses reeling. Her body crie
out for him. Nothing mattered but the need of him
She felt like a tightly wound spring, yearning fo
release. Never before in her life had she felt lik
this, wanting so much to be made love to, to giv
and be taken. She did not care about anything, onl
that he had gone from her arms, leaving her feelin
unutterably empty and unfulfilled.

Gradually, her wildly beating heart slowed an
reality returned. She could hear him movin
around on the deck, the sound of clattering chain
Swinging her bare feet to the floor, she wrapped th
blanket tightly round her and went through to th
main saloon. He was clambering down the hatch
way and turned to face her.

'What was wrong?' she asked.

'The wind had changed direction. We were drag
ging our anchor dangerously near the rocks. It's al
right now. I've put out another anchor. I shoul
have done that in the first place.'

They remained standing apart, each knowing th
other was remembering their earlier caresses. Sh
felt her heart beginning to thump again.

He cleared his throat unnecessarily and some
how it was made clear that there was to be no retur
to their previous intimacy. But why had he sudden
ly become so distant and cold? Feeling utterl
rejected, she stood there uncertainly.

'No, Katherine. You do not understand. I am not free.'

She stared at him for a moment and then turned and ran blindly from the cabin, the tears welling up in her eyes.

She threw herself on her bunk and lay there sobbing. She knew now that she was hopelessly in love with him, that she wanted to give herself to him, whether he was free or not.

CHAPTER TEN

SHE fell into a sleep of exhaustion in the early hour of the morning, having lain awake for a long time tossing and turning. Troubled images had coursed across her mind—recollections of mountainous seas, of bottomless depths of dark water and of strong arms pulling her to safety.

He had said he was not free, but surely it could not be because of Madeleine. She was so young and immature. And yet they obviously had a relationship, for she had seen him buying dresses for her. It was an intimate relationship too. One did not usually sunbathe topless in the company of a casual acquaintance. It could be simply a physical attraction, she thought miserably, for Madeleine certainly had her charms. But he would be bound to tire of someone like that very quickly. Someone in Paris, then? Giles Stephens had hinted that there was a woman in the background. He might simply be having a casual affair with Madeleine as consolation for an unhappy past. Perhaps he did not wish to subject Kate to the same shallow treatment. That at least would mean that he had a measure of respect for her. A nagging voice within, however, kept telling her that she did not want his respect. She simply wanted his love, no matter for how short a time and whatever the consequences.

She awoke to the sound of water sluicing past the hull and realised they were under way again. She looked at her watch. Ten o'clock! She dressed hurriedly in the spare clothes she had brought.

He was up on deck at the wheel.

'Good morning, Katherine,' he said lightly. 'I hope you slept well.'

'Very well, thank you,' she lied and looked around her. The mainland was a long way astern and they were heading up the coast of Corfu.

'What is happening?' she asked.

'I felt like an early start,' he replied. 'The storm rather put paid to our plans for cruising and this morning the wind is too far to the North-West to do any proper exploring. I thought we might as well make our way back to Kalami. The wind is at least in the right direction for that tack and I should really prefer to return by this evening. I have much to do in the coming week.'

He had bent down and was examining a chart with studied deliberation. She was glad, for it enabled her to conceal her disappointment. She retired down to the cabin and spent the remainder of the morning there. It was a miserable end to what should have been a fabulous weekend.

They berthed around lunchtime and Spiro came to collect her. Laurent helped her with her bag to the waiting car. He opened the rear door for her.

'Thank you for asking me, Laurent. I don't expect you bargained for what happened,' she said.

He was regarding her strangely.

'No, I certainly did not,' he replied.

'It was so silly of me to fall overboard like that.'

'Oh yes. Yes, I see.' He sounded vague, but then seemed to gather his thoughts and went on, 'I hope it has not put you off sailing.'

'No, I don't think so,' she said seriously, 'but I shall take far more care in future.'

There was an awkward silence which Kate fel
compelled to break. 'Well, all's well that ends well,
she said with artificial cheeriness. 'When will yo
be visiting Mr Jollison again?'

'Not for a while, I think. I have things I need to
attend to. But he is practically recovered, I feel
Anyway, you know where to reach me.'

'Yes, I do.'

'Well, *au revoir*, Katherine.'

She would have had no trouble keeping her
emotions under control, had he not suddenly taken
her hand, leaned forward and kissed her on the
cheek. Her eyes swam and she turned away quickly
to hide her face and slid on to the rear seat of the
Peugeot.

He must have sensed her anguish, for he simply
closed the door after her and lightly tapped the roof
of the car as a signal for Spiro to drive away. She
resisted the impulse to turn and look out of the rear
window as they accelerated away, searching frantically in her bag for a tissue.

From that day, her life at the Villa Netriti seemed
to pall. The enchantment which had touched every
aspect of her surroundings had gone, as though
some control or other had been turned from colour
to black and white. She realised, a day or two later,
that she was behaving like some love-sick teenager,
for even Mary had commented on her desponden-
cy. She hurriedly found some excuse.

'I must be getting gloomy about going back to
England, Mary. Sorry.'

'Not yet, my dear, surely. There's no need for
that. Paul and I plan to stay on until July or August
at least. He's been in correspondence with the
agency and they're managing quite well without

him, thank goodness. It's a chance to have him on my own which I haven't had for years. Nobody's indispensable in an office I keep telling him. They've even managed to run the Chantelle perfume campaign without him. That young man you know, Graham Browne, nearly ruined everything by chasing after his lady client. Paul's partner, Ed, had to fire him in the end.' Mistaking Kate's expression for one of concern, she added hastily, 'Oh, I forgot, he wasn't a special friend, was he my dear? How silly of me.'

'No, no, Mary,' smiled Kate wryly. 'Just an acquaintance.' Memories of her life in London just before departing for Corfu only served to depress her even further, however.

The weeks passed and gradually she knew she must begin planning for her return to England, despite the Jollisons' entreaties that she stay on and enjoy a holiday. She knew that the ache in her heart would not diminish as long as she stayed on this beautiful island. Her feelings for Laurent de Kerouac might become more bearable as time passed, but certainly not whilst she stayed at the Villa Netriti.

The thought that she would return began to dominate. Back to London, initially, but perhaps a return to the West Country eventually. She could easily get a post at the South Devon General again, perhaps even do another stint in Intensive Care. Getting back into some really demanding nursing was the best antidote for how she felt, she was certain.

She resolved to put these plans into action. Her return flight would be simple to arrange, for she held an open ticket. She would have to discuss it with Laurent, however, because she should really obtain his agreement that her patient no longer needed her.

Despite everything, she still could not restrain a sense of anticipation at the thought of seeing him again. Perhaps she would drop in to his surgery in Corfu Town and discuss it with him there—she wanted to go in to buy some presents anyway. She decided to go in on the bus the next day. The bus was full, for the tourist season had really arrived now. She experienced a rather self-indulgent feeling of superiority, for she knew her tan had deepened and that her fair hair had bleached almost white in the sun. She was dressed casually in jeans and sandals and recently had taken to not wearing a bra under her white cotton blouse. All the inhibitions associated with the colder English climate had gone and she felt like a local. She even found the words to ask for her ticket in Greek and made her way down the swaying aisle to a rear seat, aware of appraising eyes on her from the groups of holiday makers.

Corfu Town was much busier now and the time soon passed as she bought presents for her parents and flatmates. She had recalled that Laurent took his surgery in the evening and she began to thread her way through the streets towards the square near the harbour where his apartment was situated. As she strolled, somewhat laden down with parcels, along a line of colourful waterside bars, she heard her name being called and looked across the tables to see Giles Stephens and Jean, her hosts at that villa barbecue so long ago, beckoning to her. She negotiated her way towards them.

'Kate, what are you doing here?' said Giles, rising to his feet.

'Doing some shopping,' she replied. 'Buying presents actually.'

'So I see,' said Jean, eyeing Kate's parcels. 'You certainly believe in doing things all in one go.'

'Well, I shall be going back to England soon,' explained Kate. 'As a matter of fact I'm on my way to discuss my leaving date with Laurent now.'

'Well, you've got a long journey, then,' laughed Giles.

'Sorry?'

'He and Maddie are in Paris. Didn't you know?'

Kate stared at them.

'Maddie?' she heard herself ask. 'Paris?'

'Yes, he took Madeleine there for the weekend,' said Jean. 'I think it was a treat for her eighteenth birthday.' She smiled brightly.

Kate recoiled. One of her parcels, a leather bag for her mother, slipped from her fingers. Giles stooped to pick it up and she was grateful for the diversion, for she could feel the tears rising to her eyes. She fumbled for the sunglasses perched on top of her head and pulled them down to hide her feelings, almost losing another parcel.

Giles held out the package she had dropped. 'I'm not sure exactly when they'll be back,' he said.

'No. Of course not. Don't worry. I can see him another time,' said Kate tightly. 'Well, I must be going.'

'Won't you stay for a cup of coffee?' asked Jean.

'No, thank you. I think I'll try and make the six o'clock bus. I can just do it. Goodbye.'

She turned and stumbled hurriedly away between the tables, uncaring that her departure must have seemed hasty and ill-mannered.

'Hope we'll see you again before you leave,' she heard Giles call in a puzzled tone and summoning her very last reserve of composure, she turned and waved, forcing a smile of acknowledgement. Then she was rushing along the busy pavements, the tears running down her face unchecked.

She reached the bus terminus and thankfully found an empty seat where she subsided in a heap of parcels and bags.

Somehow, hearing the girl referred to as 'Maddie' was the worst hurt of all. Giles had said it almost in terms of affection, as though it were a well used nickname—as though she were a familiar part of Laurent's life. Obviously the relationship which the two of them shared was well known and freely accepted amongst their friends. That she had not been a party to this knowledge made Kate feel even more excluded, duped almost. How stupid she had been to even hope that she might have had some place in his life. She felt very alone.

She was hardly aware of the bus journey home and could not even bring herself to show Mary the results of her shopping trip. She made an excuse about everywhere being very hot and crowded and went to bed.

She arose the next morning, however, with a very clear head and a strong sense of purpose. It was as though some expurgation had gone on in her mind whilst she slept. The events of the last few months had taken on the quality of a dream, an interlude of exquisite unreality from which she was now emerging. After breakfast, she went over to the kitchen.

'Please will you telephone the airline for me in

Corfu Town?' she asked Spiro.

'Airline. You leave us, Kate? But Mr Jollison, the doctor, they still need you here.' Spiro's expression was of deep concern as he made these protests, translating them in excited asides for Elena's benefit.

'No,' said Kate firmly. 'It is time for me to leave. Mr Jollison is completely better. He just needs a holiday now. I must go back to my life in England. I will explain to the Jollisons and to the doctor, but first I wish to find out about flights and seats.'

She was touched by the consternation her request had caused and had to cling on to her resolve firmly. She knew that she was displaying definite signs of becoming weepy again and the only cure for that was to make firm plans to start reassembling her life.

At last she prevailed upon Spiro and he went over to the telephone. As he was about to pick it up, it rang. He lifted the receiver and a rapid exchange of Greek followed. He turned to Kate.

'It's for you,' he said. 'Sister Theresa.'

Kate gaped in astonishment. 'Sister Theresa?' she repeated.

'Yes. From Paxos.'

She took the proffered receiver. Sister Theresa's voice crackled tinnily in her ear. The static on the line was appalling, but through it Kate could hear a very different tone of voice from the nun's normal soft brogue.

'Ah, Nurse Trelawney . . . it's glad I am . . . contact you. Can't reach Dr de Kerouac.'

'Is anything wrong, Sister?' attempted Kate through the mush of electrical interference.

'The children . . . very bad gastro-enteritis . . .

Some of the sisters too . . . I'm worried about th
very young ones and little Maria especially.'

'Have they seen a doctor at all?' Kate's ears wer
straining to hear the reply.

'The doctor came from Galios . . . couldn't sta
long.'

'Would you like me to come over on the ferry an
help?'

'Oh Nurse Trelawney, if you could . . . not s
well, myself.'

'I'll be on the very next boat,' promised Kate
'Don't worry.'

She replaced the receiver, her mind switching
into top gear. If they hurried, she could catch th
same ferry she and Laurent had taken that time—
the ten o'clock. Within minutes, she had despatch
ed Spiro to get the car out, had explained th
emergency to the Jollisons and was hurriedl
throwing things into her bag. She hesitated, the
added her ward dress, apron and cap. She would
travel in her denim skirt and cotton blouse.

She made the ferry just in time and sped up th
gangplank as the mooring ropes were being unfas
tened. The boat was full of tourists, all clicking
cameras and clutching guide books. She fel
strangely aloof and found a quiet corner away from
the babble.

She steadfastly refused to dwell on the memory
of her last crossing on this ferry and applied he
mind to the practical issues which lay ahead. Gas
tro-enteritis was usually only very serious amongs
extremely young infants, whose limited reserves o
water meant dehydration was the principle prob
lem. Presumably though, the sisters would be
aware of the need to provide as much fluid as

possible for the children. She was not really sure to what extent she would be needed at the orphanage, but had enough experience to know that in any crisis a fresh pair of healthy hands were always welcome. And Sister Theresa would not have telephoned unless she really needed help. At last she felt a change in the vibrations of the ship's engines under her feet and she went up to join the group of excited tourists at the bow as they slipped through the cliffs into the cove at Lacca. Despite herself, her eyes were drawn to where *Liberté* had been moored on that first trip and she felt a pang at seeing the spot looking so empty.

Sister Theresa swung open the wooden gate to greet her with an expression of acute relief. Her face was grey and drawn and she was nothing like the effervescent soul Kate had first met.

'It is so good of you to come, Nurse Trelawney. It has been a long night. Some of the children have been very poorly.'

Kate rested a hand on the nun's arm.

'It's the least I can do, Sister Theresa,' she said kindly. 'I'll just get changed and then we'll see what I can help with. It looks to me as though you need some rest. Just how much sleep have you had?'

'Enough, Nurse, but thank you. Come along this way, we've a spare room you can use.'

Within a very short time Kate had assessed the situation. Since there appeared to be no common element of diet, except perhaps the water, the trouble must have been caused by a virus. The sisters had taken all the sensible measures to contain it—separate towels for everybody and extra careful washing of utensils and crockery. Those

who were only mildly affected had been put on a
diet of plain boiled rice.

The real cause for concern was little Maria. She
lay in bed, her knees drawn up and in obvious pain
from stomach spasms.

Kate sat on the edge of her bed and gently
stroked the hair back from the child's forehead.

'It's backwards and forwards I've been to the
toilet with her all night, Nurse. She's exhausted.'

'And so are you, Sister. You said the doctor
came from Gaios this morning. What did he say?'

'He gave her an injection to ease the spasms.
Here.' Sister Theresa was examining some notes on
a pad. She held them out to Kate.

'Ah yes. An alkaloid shot. Well, that would have
helped, but she must be very dehydrated now.' A
thought struck her. 'What happened with that
blood test we took?'

'Oh, Dr de Kerouac rang through to say it was
negative. She must have just picked up a minor
infection. The trouble is it's left her very run down
and not in a good state for this upset.'

'That's right enough,' mused Kate. 'Well, I think
the most important thing now is for you to get some
rest, Sister. I shall sit here and keep an eye on
Maria, encourage her to take some fluids.'

'She's not keeping much down, Nurse.'

'Well, you leave things to me and look after
yourself a little. Is the doctor from Gaios coming
again?'

'Not today, I'm afraid. Perhaps tomorrow. It's
rushed off his feet he was, poor man.'

'I see.' Kate pursed her lips and hid her concern,
for the child was obviously very poorly. It was
essential to get some fluids into her. She rose to her

feet and insisted that Sister Theresa retired immediately.

As the afternoon wore on, it became clear that Maria was incapable of taking even the boiled water which Sister Theresa had prepared. Kate's concern grew, for it was obvious that she was becoming very weak. She was lying prostrate, her breathing becoming more shallow by the minute. She needed salt as well, but her stomach had become so conditioned to spasm that it was impossible for her to retain anything long enough to absorb it. The real answer was an anti-emetic. Kate had brought an assortment of drugs, including chalk and opium mixtures, but what was missing was some chlorpromazine.

Suddenly she remembered the pharmacy cabinet in the room which Laurent used as a surgery. She sped along the stone corridors and stairs. She quickly found the key in his desk drawer and opened the cabinet. Her eyes scanned the collection of bottles and jars and alighted on one marked Largactil, the drug held in fluid suspension. She should be able to administer it orally.

She rushed back to Maria's room and, lifting the child's head, gently coaxed her to take a teaspoonful. She swallowed, grimacing at the taste, and Kate cradled her, willing her to retain the medicine. Minutes passed and Kate began to relax. She gently lowered her back on to the pillow and checked her watch. In an hour she would try her with a proper drink. She remained on the edge of the bed holding the little girl's hand in hers, softly comforting her.

Maria tossed and turned, whimpering occasionally and Kate kept applying a cool wet cloth to her forehead. After a time she began to moisten her lips with some of the boiled water, using some cotton wool as a sponge. It seemed as though the chlorpromazine was having an effect, for her restless movements began to lessen.

By dusk, Kate knew she had won. At hourly intervals she had been able to increase Maria's intake of water until on the most recent occasion she had managed to switch her to a saline solution. She was sleeping now, her legs no longer drawn up in spasm and she was clutching the large teddy bear which was apparently her constant companion. Just before she drifted off to sleep, she had rewarded Kate with a smile, a little faint perhaps, but nevertheless one of great affection.

Kate lit the large candle nightlight on the bedside table and sat back in her chair with a feeling of intense relief. She felt a great sense of satisfaction, for she knew she had correctly analysed the situation and taken the right action. This was one of the great fulfilments of nursing, she reflected, knowing you could give help to a person when they were helpless themselves. Getting thoroughly involved in a proper nursing job again would be a very good thing—in fact an essential thing to blur the unrealities of her brief spell on Corfu. And yet, she knew very well that her feelings for Laurent were very real indeed and that she would never be able to forget him completely.

She must have dozed, for as if from a great way off she became aware of a hand gently but firmly shaking her shoulder.

'She's sleeping now, Sister Theresa. It's all right,' she murmured and opened her eyes. It was dark, the room lit by the wan glow from the nightlight.

The deeper shadows in the corners were flickering, or there was a draught where the door had been left open.

Not a hand's breadth from her eyes was Laurent's face, regarding her with such an expression of tenderness and concern that her heart turned over. She sat up abruptly.

'Laurent! But you're in Paris,' she exclaimed. He hastened a finger to his lips, looking sideways at the sleeping child.

'I came to help,' she whispered. 'Maria has been very ill.'

He nodded seriously and went over to the bedside to observe the child more closely. Kate rose and joined him.

'How long have you been here?' she asked, still somewhat stunned at the manner of his arrival.

'I caught the evening ferry. It was delayed with engine trouble or I would have been here sooner.'

They stood together, looking down at the sleeping child. Kate was very aware of him at her side. Despite everything, she knew she was very pleased indeed to see him. He turned to her and she realised she had been staring at him. His face looked drawn and there was a slight hint of fatigue in his expression, but it passed as he caught her gaze and his eyes softened in a smile.

'She seems calm now. There is a colour to her cheeks and she is breathing deeply,' he observed quietly.

'Yes, she's not so dehydrated now. I managed to get her to take an anti-emetic.'

He picked up the bottle of Largactil.

'It seems to have done the trick,' he smiled.

'Yes, it has.' She paused. 'You don't look surprised to see me, Laurent.'

'Oh, I'm not. My surgery told me that Sister
Theresa had been asking for you to come over so I
rang your villa and Spiro explained. I'm glad you
were able to come. So is Sister. She said she was
very relieved to see you.'

'Well, it was the very least I could do,' replied
Kate. 'But you haven't been troubling her, have
you? She's absolutely exhausted.'

'She answered my ring at the door,' he explained
apologetically and then added hastily, 'Don't worry. I've packed her back off to bed. She told me I'd
find you here.'

Maria stirred in her sleep and they froze.

The child's movement had caused the teddy bear
to fall across her face and Kate gently moved it to
one side and straightened the sheets. She started as
Laurent bent towards her, his mouth close to her
ear.

'Come. I must talk with you,' he breathed.

She allowed him to take her hand and lead her
gently from the room. There was no thought of not
complying and she went almost meekly.

Any resolve she had built to treat him with
indifference when next she saw him scattered like
spray before the wind. There was a dream-like
quality about everything—the flickering candle
light, the hushed tones in which they had been
talking and the silence of their passing from the
room. For an absurd moment she had the notion
that she was imagining it all, but the firm pressure
of his hand on hers was real enough and she allowed
him to guide her along the stone-flagged corridors.
He led her into a large courtyard and over to a

wooden bench set against an ancient moss-covered wall. The building was bathed in moonlight, the shadows silent and reflective. She felt her heart beginning to thump.

He took both her hands now and lightly pressed her to sit on the bench. He settled beside her. She could not see his features clearly, for the moonlight had thrown them into shadow. He had not let go of her hands and she knew she was not going to withdraw them.

'Katherine,' he said softly. 'You must realise that I have fallen in love with you.'

It was as if the moment were frozen in time; as though the image of them sitting together on the bench in the moonlit courtyard had been focused on her memory by some strange camera and he had pressed the shutter.

'I never thought it would happen again, but it has,' he said simply. 'I want you, Katherine, here with me in Greece, to be my wife. I believe I have loved you from the moment you practically fell into my arms that day in London. It seems a lifetime ago. But I knew for certain when I nearly lost you off *Liberté* in the storm. I wanted to make love to you so much that night.'

She stared at him, her mouth dry.

'But Laurent, you have just been to Paris for a—weekend with Madeleine.'

'It was just a birthday present,' he said. Good heavens, he almost sounded resentful. 'She always tries to visit her mother on her birthday.'

'Her mother?' Kate's eyes widened in astonishment. 'You took her to visit her mother?'

'Yes.' He sounded puzzled. 'My ex-wife, that is.'

Suddenly the pieces of a jigsaw moved together

in Kate's mind. Could it be? It would explain the easy, close relationship which the two of them obviously enjoyed. Almost scared to ask the question, she leaned forward, her eyes widening incredulously.

'You mean Madeleine's your *daughter*?'

'Yes, she is. And quite a handful, I can tell you. You may have noticed. I could do with some help with her.'

'But she's so young—I mean old,' she added in confusion. 'I thought—but why did nobody tell me? And you said you weren't free. I don't understand.'

He clasped her hands between his.

'I was married very young, Kate. It could never have lasted and I was divorced years ago. But I promised myself I would not get involved with anyone else until Maddie was eighteen. I was awarded custody of her in the divorce and she's never really got on with her mother. That's why she lives out here in Greece with me. She only sees her mother once or twice a year—on birthdays for example.'

Kate was speechless. She felt a great wave of exultation rising but dared not let it break over her. His face was in shadow, but she was positive it wore an expression of agonised suspense.

'Please, say something, Katherine,' he implored.

'Oh Laurent, I was so confused about you and Maddie. I kept seeing you together and I thought . . .' She trailed off, lost for words.

'You surely did not think Maddie and I were—?'

'I did not know what to think. I knew you wanted to make love to me on *Liberté* that night and I wanted you to, but then when you—'

'What did you say, Katherine?'

'I said I knew you wanted to make love to me that night.'

'No, I meant what you said after that.'

She was silent, wanting to blush, cry and laugh all at the same time. Laurent was leaning towards her.

'You said you wanted me to make love to you,' he said.

'Yes, Laurent, I did.'

'Like this?' he asked gently, and lightly brushed her lips with his. She could sense he was smiling and she matched his mood.

'A little like that,' she agreed. 'In fact, quite a lot like that.'

He took her in his arms and kissed her again. She let the wave of exultation sweep right over her. This time she knew there would be no going back.